TONGUES OF ANGELS

Also by Julia Park Tracey

The Doris Diaries series

I've Got Some Lovin' to Do: The Diaries of a Roaring Twenties Teen (1925-1926), Indie-Visible Ink, 2012

Reaching for the Moon: More Diaries of a Roaring Twenties Teen (1927-1929), Indie-Visible Ink, 2013

***

Confessions: Fact or Fiction,
Edited by Herta Feely and Marion Wernicke;
Chrysalis Editorial, 2010

Amaryllis: Collected Poems, Scarlet Letter Press, 2009

Reading Harry Potter: Critical Essays,
Edited by Giselle Anatol; Praeger, 2003

TONGUES OF ANGELS
A NOVEL

Copyright © 2013 Julia Park Tracey.

All rights reserved. No part of this book may be used or reproduced by any means, graphic, electronic, or mechanical, including photocopying, recording, taping or by any information storage retrieval system without the written permission of the publisher except in the case of brief quotations embodied in critical articles and reviews.

This is a work of fiction. All of the characters, names, incidents, organizations, and dialogue in this novel are either the products of the author's imagination or are used fictitiously.

iUniverse books may be ordered through booksellers or by contacting:

iUniverse
1663 Liberty Drive
Bloomington, IN 47403
www.iuniverse.com
1-800-Authors (1-800-288-4677)

Because of the dynamic nature of the Internet, any web addresses or links contained in this book may have changed since publication and may no longer be valid. The views expressed in this work are solely those of the author and do not necessarily reflect the views of the publisher, and the publisher hereby disclaims any responsibility for them.

ISBN: 978-1-4759-8570-2 (sc)
ISBN: 978-1-4759-8572-6 (hc)
ISBN: 978-1-4759-8571-9 (e)

Library of Congress Control Number: 2013906683

Printed in the United States of America

iUniverse rev. date: 4/29/2013

First edition © 2003 by Julia Park
Second revised edition
© 2013 by Julia Park Tracey

Originally published as
Tongues of Angels: A Novel by Julia Park
ISBN 0595278205
Scarlet Letter Press, Alameda, California, 2003

Cover graphics by Chelsea Starling

Indie-Visible Ink
www.indie-visible.com
Birmingham Charlottesville Nashville
San Francisco Seattle Sydney Tauranga

Tongues of Angels

A Novel

Julia Park Tracey

Indie-Visible Ink

iUniverse, Inc.
Bloomington

What critics are saying about *Tongues of Angels*

Jordan Rosenfeld, *Forged in Grace*: "Julia Park Tracey brings wicked honesty and scathingly hot prose to this soulful novel; with crackling nuance, she seduces readers. *Tongues of Angels* is both sexy and spiritual."

David Baker, *Red Hills Review*: "(A) comic novel about masculinity…the main characters, California Catholic priests, are manipulated by lust like puppets from the ropes of their cassocks. The closest contemporary work of fiction is Jeanette Winterson's *Oranges Are Not the Only Fruit*… (A)s erotically compelling as the *Song of Songs*."

Christa Martin, *Good Times/Santa Cruz*: "It lifts up the chasuble…and exposes what's underneath. Her story talks about all the things that some Catholics are hoping we won't talk about…"

Dan Barnett, *Chico Enterprise-Record*: "Sexually charged: I was struck by [Park Tracey's] lush, hothouse, erotic style."

Kelly Vance, *East Bay Express*: "Hot under the collar…A scandalous yarn."

Woody Minor, *Alameda at Play*: "Julia Park Tracey has crafted a fine and funny novel that takes the reader inside the priesthood — and the priest — to reveal the all-too-human side of the Catholic Church. Highly recommended."

To my lovely daughters

Tongues of Angels

A Novel

If I speak in the tongues of men and of angels, I am a noisy gong or a clanging cymbal. If I have the gift of prophecy and, with full knowledge, comprehend all mysteries, I have faith great enough to move mountains, but have not love, I am nothing.
—1 Corinthians 13:1-2

"*I have never encountered a sexual problem that was not also a religious problem, nor a religious problem that was not also a sexual problem.*"
—C.G. Jung

Contents

Prologue 1
Ordinary Time 5
Advent 35
Christmas 51
Ordinary Time 65
Lent 99
Holy Week 129
Triduum 139
Easter 153
Pentecost 179
Ordinary Time 205

A Reader's Guide to *Tongues of Angels* 219

Prologue

On feast days he wore red, the blood red of virgin martyrs and cardinals. His brocade chasuble, a heavy mantle that draped him from his collar to his shoes, was piped with gold, curved at the hem, with a slit for his head. When he walked he seemed to glide, and when he held his hands out to consecrate the Eucharist, the chasuble shifted to reveal his arms, cloaked in white from the linen alb he wore underneath, exposing the narrow cuffs of his black clerical shirt beneath the alb, layer under layer that ended at the naked brown skin of his hands.

Father Robert Souza was a Roman Catholic priest, under the chasuble and alb, and clerical collar (size Pontiff 3) and the black shirt and slacks that are the uniform of the priest.

And under that, boxer shorts.

And under those, the man.

Rob had deliberated over the boxers. For years he had worn bleached white shorts that his mother had ironed, yes, ironed with a heavy hand and an ancient iron that she ran over paraffin for a crisp sheen. When he was old enough to buy his own shorts, he switched to tight, bright bikini briefs, which had amused his fellow seminarians and given him adolescent moments in front of the mirror, admiring his physique, a blue-collar Portuguese boy in Speedos, building muscles to lift a chalice. His former girlfriend had once given him some black silk boxers which he still kept but never wore; after ordination, Rob bought white briefs that somehow conferred respectability with their simple, practical function, and suited his position in the parish.

But when Rob visited with some parishioners who suffered infertility problems, the husband explained how briefs lowered his sperm count and how, that for healthy sperm, a man should wear looser shorts. Rob worked through the issue as if it were a syllogism, a geometric proof: *If tight shorts lower the sperm count, and lower sperm count can affect fertility, then men should wear loose shorts to ensure fertility.* But when he added the *x* factor of celibate priesthood into the equation, he faltered. He didn't need a sperm count, high or low. Rob stood before the underwear display in a department store on his day off, anonymous and average in his jeans and chambray shirt, and weighed his decision.

When a man has a vocation to the priesthood, he must meet certain qualifications to be ordained: be at least twenty-four years old, a legitimate child, and of sound mind and body, although the Bishop could dispense most impediments. Rob himself had received a dispensation from the Bishop because he had been a few months shy of his twenty-fourth birthday at his ordination six years before, and one of Rob's classmates received a dispensation because of an undescended testicle. St. Thomas Aquinas had preached, long before the invention of the microscope, that each drop of a man's seed was like a tiny man, thus sacred, and despite more modern medical understanding, the Catholic doctrine was the same. Although a priest must never put his gift to use, the living seed must be cherished. Rob, sound of mind and body, poised to choose between the guilty freedom of boxer shorts versus the ball-crushing, sperm-killing snap of tight elastic, was glad to have worked it out.

He had worn boxers ever since.

Ordinary Time

CHAPTER ONE

Rob searched the crowd in the Italian restaurant for a friend. His sun-darkened skin was bronze against his white collar. He felt the heat through his many layers, the weight of black clericals on an August day, the rub of his collar on his brown neck, and wished himself again on the soft shore of Kauai, with cool-warm water lapping his toes, an iced drink at hand. But vacation was over, summer almost gone, and the pace of church life about to pick up dramatically. Rob cupped a hand to his eyes to see across the outside courtyard, where tables were set under an awning, and patrons lounged with wine glasses at the outdoor bar.

There, Rob spied the sun-bleached hair, heard the distinct laugh, recognized at once the erect posture of his best friend, Father Lawrence Poole, bantering with the bartender. They hadn't seen each other all summer; Lawrence had been in Italy for a month, then Rob had gone to Hawaii to visit relatives. Rob had missed Lawrence more than he'd expected, felt the loss of the regular afternoon call which filled that empty portion of the day; he had missed Lawrence's wicked laughter through the phone line, the gossip and the companionship that only two souls with the same vocation could know.

Lawrence greeted Rob with a hug. "Hey, there, sweetie. You look relaxed. Did you get lucky over the summer?"

"Ha, ha." Rob hugged Lawrence back. "You're projecting. Is there something you need to confess?"

Lawrence put his hand over his heart and made a tragic face. "My lips are sealed." Lawrence kissed his fingertips, eyes closed reverently.

"I'll bet."

The maitre d' arrived to escort them to a table.

As Rob and Lawrence passed through the restaurant, a lingering trace of perfume met them, to Rob, as familiar as the scent of his own pillow, his own warmed bed, sweet and musky as a woman. And there was a woman somewhere in the room, nameless, anointed with a certain scent, one that pulled him like a ribbon of memory. Another woman had worn the same perfume for him, long ago; a fragrance forever associated with her, that time, that place, that choice, leading down to this moment, this life. Rob pushed the thought back as they came to their table, and he took his seat. A waitress stood by to take their order.

"Have a drink with me," Lawrence said, dropping into his chair. "I want to celebrate."

"Let's get a bottle, then," said Rob, taking up the wine list. He pointed to a Sonoma Chardonnay. "This one's fine," he told their waitress. As he spoke to her, he noticed a fading red mark—knife slice, cat scratch? —on the back of her hand.

The young waitress in her black trousers and crisp white shirt noted the wine and nodded. Rob handed her the list, watching the curve of her jaw as she walked away, the one brown strand of hair at the nape of her white neck that her hair clasp had missed. He made himself look around the restaurant, noticing instead the marble counters, the open windows where the breeze came in, and the terra cotta tile of the floor.

"Tell me what we're celebrating," Rob said.

"Ah. Yes. Something wonderful." Lawrence smiled, his face still glowing with a Southern California tan, sun-bleached bangs that he tossed from his forehead like an impatient colt. "I met a man last month when I was home in La Jolla for a few days."

"Oh, don't tell me—you're in love." Rob covered his ears.

"Oh, no, nothing like that."

"Thank God."

The waitress returned with the bottle of wine. Rob watched her strong hands as she presented the chill green bottle, deftly opened it, poured, and left them again. When Rob had attended St. Joseph's Seminary, the nuns who had cared for them—washed the seminarians' clothes, cooked and served the meals—had belonged to a cloistered order. They never showed their faces, but worked silently in the refectory behind a screen, raised just enough to push out plates of food, with only their hands visible. He recalled their unadorned hands, some freckled with liver spots and others blue-veined with age. One particular pair of hands was youthful, smooth and slender, the color of coffee ice cream, with short squared nails. Rob's first years at seminary had been a torment, dreaming of those hands.

Rob had never stopped yearning. He knew desire that could sweep through him: the untwisting of a tourniquet, the full heat of blood that floods into a pallid limb, the deliberate twist again to stop the flow. He coped with Zen-like mantras, a Hindu's control of the physical self, a Jewish sense of guilt. Rob tasted the wheat-colored wine, letting its crisp-tart flavor lie on his tongue before he swallowed its coolness. "So what about this guy?"

Lawrence swirled the wine in his glass and held it to the light to admire its pale color. His long tapered fingers, as if shaped in the womb just to play piano, curved gracefully around the stem of the glass. "It turns out this guy works for Archangel Records. I told him about my plan to compose a Mass, and he was interested." Lawrence had often talked of composing the Propers for an entire Mass.

"Well, so, he's interested, so what? That means nothing. I gave him my number and flew back up here, thinking, shot in the dark, chance in a million he'll call me. My typical luck." Lawrence sipped his wine. "But this week he actually called. He connected me with this agent in L.A. who handles church music, and they gave me a deadline. I have till June 1 to compose the music, score it, arrange it, make the demo, and get the package to them. And *if* I make the deadline, and *if* they like it, we'll record it. I'll have a Mass out for liturgical use—and royalties, I hasten to add. Not bad, huh?" He raised an eyebrow.

"You lead a charmed life." Rob clinked his glass to Lawrence's. "What'll you do with the money?"

"Give it to Mother Church, of course. Use it to fund some music ministries—like maybe a new cathedral choir."

"They do need help."

Lawrence sighed. "But there's a problem."

"What?"

"There are only two priests at Resurrection, and we're both booked solid with meetings every night and weddings every Saturday. I have no free time to compose now. The timing is awful! Autumn is the worst, you know, with all these activities, and next thing you know, boom, it's Advent, Christmas, then it's Lent, and where's the time gone?" Lawrence jerked his thumb over his shoulder. "Out the window with my recording contract. If the timing was different, I'd be fine. I *can't* pass this up, but I don't know how I'm going to make it, either."

"Why don't I take some of your weddings? Let me know the dates," Rob offered, as their entrees arrived. The waitress leaned against him, a brush, a nudge, as she worked; setting plates before them, grinding pepper, offering Parmesan, smooth and efficient. Rob and Lawrence waited until she walked away, and then they bowed their heads for a silent prayer. They began to eat.

"So Italy was good?" Rob asked, blowing on a forkful of steaming pasta.

Lawrence held his hand to his heart again. "The best. It always is. I should move there. I will, someday." He sighed. "How was Hawaii?"

"Hot." Rob remembered the warm wind, the heat of white sand at his back. "I just lay around at the beach most of the time."

"Oh?" Lawrence paused, his fork halfway to his mouth. "And?"

"And I got a nice tan. End of story."

"I'll hear your confession later, my son."

"You're a real funny guy, you know that?" Rob gave Lawrence a look. "Hysterical. Of course I was good."

"Nothing less than perfection from St. Robert, virgin martyr."

"Give me a break."

Lawrence crossed his fingers as if to ward off a vampire. "Next you'll tell me the 'Poor Celibate Rob' story again."

"Oh, bite me." Rob grinned as he twirled another forkful of pasta.

"You just have to get over it, Rob. You made your choice. Offer it up."

Rob reached to pour the wine, but the waitress stopped at the table and took the bottle, poured more wine into their empty glasses. Rob thanked her, his eyes on her hands, that red scratch, the bottle firm in her clasp.

"No confession, huh?" Lawrence rested his chin on his fist, and grinned at Rob.

"'Fraid not."

They sat back as a busboy cleared their plates. Lawrence's eyes followed the slender young man as he carried the plates away. Lawrence turned back to find Rob watching him. Rob clucked his tongue at his friend.

The waitress, returning with their coffee, smiled sweetly at Rob. He looked away, knowing that he must seem rude.

When she departed, Lawrence said, "She could have been another chip off your chalice."

Rob, silent, poured the last of the wine.

CHAPTER TWO

The black Jeep's tires crunched stray gravel as Rob pulled into his parking spot in back of St. Justin Martyr. No lights glowed in the large ranch-style house that was the rectory, because he was its sole occupant. Rob missed the sense of other people in the house—the TV left on, a gentle tread on the stairs—and the woman he had loved and left behind.

The sore was still there, though seldom probed. But that wisp of perfume in the restaurant, the waitress's pale neck, the memory of the nun's hands—they conspired to remind him of Shannon tonight. She lingered in his mind, her eyelids half-lowered over blue eyes, sleepy, sensual, her mouth ready to be kissed, the strap of her dress falling down. In his mind he pulled up the strap with a finger. *No, Shannon, I can't.*

Rob had decamped from his widowed mother's house at seventeen, fled her words that always cut as hard in pidgin English as in Portuguese, and ran to the open arms of Church. It was an easy decision to make back then; his father had died when Rob was ten, and the parish priests stepped in to fill the role. At their urging, he gave himself to the seminary, and later, to a priestly life. As young as Rob was, the seminary took him, educated him, taught him manners and how to speak well, made a man from the graceless boy.

Celibacy was an issue to him then, of course, a healthy boy with a healthy libido. He had given up his right to a wife at the kitchen table when he signed the application papers for the seminary, though he had plenty of opportunity to change his mind. The Church said they didn't want priests who cheated, and tried to root out the unworthy along the way. And the nun's hands were in his thoughts, he could not deny it. But how could Rob betray his intention when the most complete moments of his life had been in prayer, in the transcendent moment when the Body of Christ melted on his tongue, or in the tender release that came, every Saturday, after he had spilled his sin in the dark confessional? He thought himself strong enough to sacrifice.

In his third year of graduate school at the seminary, Rob was assigned to work in a parish in the affluent suburbs along the Peninsula south of San Francisco. The internship was part of the seminarians' supervised ministry. There he worked in the office, helped out at the parish festival, and shadowed the priest during Mass. Rob watched and learned. He listened as the choir sang. And he noticed a young woman with short blonde hair and clear Irish skin who sang with the choir.

Shannon's hands were pale and she wore no ring. She fixed her blue eyes on him as she sang the *Agnus Dei* and recited *Our Fathers*. Watching her, his heart beat faster, and he sweated under his alb. But what was the danger in drinking coffee together after Mass? What difference could an innocent lunch make? A movie was a harmless two hours in the dark. Laughter protected him from plunging in, until he found himself in her bed, the sheets twisted and damp, his denial enfleshed in her. He collapsed, his face in her neck, and squeezed his eyes closed against the sting of sweat. It had happened. He had done it. So much for celibacy.

When seminary classes ended, he was free for the summer, with no other obligations than his summer job waiting tables. He was only bending rules, not breaking them. He wasn't ordained yet, and had made no promises. What kind of priest would he make if he had never loved before? How else could he test his faith than by setting it aside for a while? Rob fooled himself until he realized that he was in love, enough in love to give him pause over the word *vocation*. And he wondered what, then, was he going to do?

Shannon came from old banking money; there was no other way to say it—she had always had money and Rob had not. Her parents welcomed Rob into their lovely home. Rob went gladly, but inside, he was a homeboy, a rube who didn't know which fork to use. He didn't dare bring Shannon home, or even mention her to his Ma. He cringed at his mother's ignorance and prejudices, her sharp criticisms. He blushed to think of Shannon sitting on that shabby sofa, seeing his mother's assemblage of plaster saints and dried-out palm leaves crowding the tabletops, feeling the brunt of that old, critical piety.

At least Shannon had faith in him. She expected him to go on and finish graduate school, to make something of himself. But when summer ended, Rob didn't go back to class. He didn't answer phone calls from his vocation director. Someone else took his room at the seminary.

Instead, Rob quit the restaurant and got a part-time job as a PE teacher at a private elementary school. He spent half-days leading calisthenics and demonstrating how to shoot a basket. In October, his classmates were ordained as deacons, the next step toward the priesthood, and made their promise of celibacy. He lay in bed with Shannon, unable to make himself get out and go, support his friends, brothers in Christ, embrace them. Face them. Say goodbye.

He and Shannon had merged into a couple, into a synchronized unit. He marveled at how their two selves melded, their boundaries blurred, like watching a science film backward, how the divided amoeba adheres and becomes one. *Rob and Shannon* began to sound like a single word, its pauses, its breathing space elided. And before he could propose to her, he realized it was already done, that she assumed they would marry, and that everyone believed them engaged.

But could he go on into marriage? Rob felt a reluctance, more than just cold feet, that he couldn't explain to her. His vocation was a forbidden topic that he couldn't broach. Rob felt paralyzed between his choices, if choices they were. Could he refuse his call? He thought of Moses, Jeremiah, a tradition of reluctant accomplices. If he married, would there always be this other voice, this other hand, tapping at his shoulder, *what about Me, why didn't you come when I called?* And if he went into the realm of the Church, he would have to leave Shannon forever, the magnitude of *forever* like an ocean, a sky, an empty room without her, without her, into Church, into the priestly life. His heart was given to both as between two lovers, no choice but to cleave himself, give half to the one and let the other half die.

One afternoon Shannon went up to the City with friends. Rob, his afternoon empty before him, walked to the parish church and knelt in its familiar hush. The sanctuary, cool and dim, cavernous and red with brick and tile, seemed to cradle him, womb-like. The Virgin of Guadalupe gazed down on him in her green gown, her mosaic face as loving and maternal to him as she had been to the Mexican peasant who first beheld her.

Kneeling, Rob felt a strange sensation grow upon him, a pricking at his soul that he couldn't shrug away, as if someone were staring at him. On the altar for Benediction, he saw the gilded, baroque monstrance with the consecrated Host inside, a pure white circle encased in glass and gold like a specimen. He gazed at the Host, exposed, and it seemed that it returned his gaze, penetrated his mind like God's own eye, and Rob remembered the simple meditation prayer, "I look at Him and He looks at me." A piercing love like a physical pain, a sense of breathless crushing ecstasy, sharper, more gripping than his own climax, ran through him, and he said out loud, "Don't—I can't take it. I can't do it." His words hung in the silence, and then the answer came like a whisper. *Can't you?*

Rob thought of Shannon, of the comfort she promised him. But he was seized again by desire for that union with God, and he began to pray all the rote prayers and utterances he had learned as a child: the *Hail Mary*, the *Our Father*, the *Confiteor*, the *Creed*. And every word rang out for him, with a newness of meaning and intent, as if he had authored them himself, and he understood where he needed to be. The only path was through the Church; the portal was the priesthood. He was Catholic; there was no other way.

But he had waited too long, had taken it too far with Shannon. He had failed her, been weighed in the balance, and found wanting. Rob remembered the curse of vocation: that if you don't have it, nothing can ever bring it to you, and if you have a vocation, no matter how you hate it, you can never escape what God has planned. He knelt at the rail in the empty church and shivered, felt the burn of tears on his face, and knew at last how much he was giving up for God.

Rob closed the door softly when he arrived at Shannon's apartment that evening. She worked in the blue-tiled kitchen with her French copper pans and bunches of herbs, a pot simmering on the stove, the table set, musky perfume on her skin. She curved a smile to welcome him home.

Rob stood watching her, his eyes on her small white hands, his brown ones fisted in his pockets. "We have to talk; I have to tell you something."

Shannon slipped her arms around him. "What is it?" Rob kept his hands in his pockets. Shannon pulled away. "Is something wrong?"

He took a long breath, felt his face redden. "I don't know how else to say it. I hardly can." He forced himself. "I'm going back to the seminary to finish my degree."

"So you've decided to finish up. Good for you." She watched him warily, her arms crossed on her chest.

"And then I'll be ordained."

"As a deacon, right?" *Don't tell me this. Don't go there*, she seemed to say.

"Yes—then as a priest."

"A priest? You're joking, right?" She half-laughed, though her face was ashen.

Rob stood silently.

"A Catholic priest?" As if she wasn't Catholic herself, had never heard of such a thing.

"Yes." Rob watched the color bloom up her face.

"A *celibate* Catholic priest."

Rob nodded.

"Well, what about me? What about our life together? Or is that too obvious?" He saw how blue her eyes were against the blush. "After all our plans—how could you do this?"

"Shan, I don't know. It's just something I have to do. God, if you only knew, I don't want it to be this way. How I wish it was different." His words whined in his ears. "I can't have both you and the Church."

"But you've made your choice, right?" She jerked away.

"I wish it were as simple as that. But it's not; it's as if the choice was made for me." He wanted to hold her, but he couldn't, he shouldn't now.

"You must have known all along. But you never said a thing about it. Why couldn't you come to me, tell me?" She abruptly began to stack dishes in the sink, clattering, clanking, sluicing water in a heavy bowl.

"Shan, it's bigger than me and what I want." Rob searched for better words, but failed. "How can I say no to God?"

She dropped the bowl with a crash in the sink. The heavy pottery broke into jagged pieces. She turned around, crumbling into sobs. "How can I even begin to compete with God? The contest is over—that's it—I lose!" She came back to him, put her arms around him. "Rob, please don't do this—there are other things you can do, youth ministry, or teach catechism, or something. We can do it together, whatever it is. But don't push me out, don't push me away. Don't leave."

Her tears made him hate himself, hate God, hate the words that he had to say. He wrapped her close to him, felt every sob shudder through her body. "I'm so sorry."

She pulled away, her eyes rimmed in red. She wiped her wet face with the back of her hand. "Rob, I love you. I want you. I want to be married, and have children, and a life together. Babies in my arms. Someone in my bed. That kind of love my whole life." She gazed at him, warm, yearning, everything he needed in her. "Together we could have all those things. But if you do this, if you go through with this, *you won't*. All you'll have is a depressing, empty rectory and long, lonesome nights. You'll be a lonely man, your whole life. Is that what you want instead of me?"

"No," he said. "But I have to go."

Robert Manuel Souza was ordained a year later at Holy Trinity Cathedral.

Rob found antacid in a cupboard and popped two tablets into his mouth. He flipped through a magazine in the living room, but nothing interested him. The air conditioner blew cool air with a gentle whirr. Rob sat down in an armchair and thought of Shannon again, and how she would laugh, or maybe cry, to see him, alone in the stillness of the rectory, her prophecy fulfilled.

The rectory settled around him. Cars whooshed by on the dark street. From a nearby yard, a dog barked. The emptiness had a hollow, nameless sound all its own. Rob sat alone in his chair and recalled the red slash like a warning flag on the waitress's hand, how she held the long bottle firm in her grasp, and released the cork in one long stroke.

CHAPTER THREE

On a Tuesday night in September, Rob's RCIA class met at St. Justin Martyr for the first time to begin the nine-month-long program for adults who wanted to become Catholic. *The Rite of Christian Initiation for Adults* was the program's official title, but everyone knew it by its initials. Rob thought of the nine months as a gestation period of sorts. He took the inquisitive minds of the seekers, the spiritually needy, and drew a frame of reference for them, filled the frame with history, elemental theology, an outline of Catholic culture. What to do, how to say, what it all means. And *why*. At the end of the nine months, he heard each one's first confession, anointed them with the oil of Confirmation, gave each one the first taste of the Body and Blood of Christ, and made Catholics of them.

The strangers gathered in the vestibule around the small table, where volunteers greeted them and handed out neon-colored nametags. Rob recognized some of their faces: a young man who had never been baptized, and the Protestant wife of a couple he'd recently married. Another woman came through the door, and more people followed. They stood around the vestibule, talking in shy murmurs, their nametags garish on shirts and blouses.

"May I have everyone's attention, please? Let's move into the gathering room so we can get started," Rob said, his voice projecting into the high ceiling of the vestibule. The group crowded through the double doors to the gathering room and took seats in a semicircle of folding chairs that faced the podium. Rob went to the front as people settled themselves. He counted thirty-two heads, including his six volunteers, and wrote the number in precise printing on a yellow legal pad. Index cards with his outlined notes rested at the side of the podium. Rob pressed his fingers into the sides, compressing the cards into a solid rectangular block.

"I want to thank you for coming tonight," he said, looking around the semicircle. "The process of initiation into the Catholic Church is a very special one, and it will be different for each of you. Part of our faith journey is becoming a *community*." He emphasized the word. "The RCIA community is a part of the parish of St. Justin's. St. Justin's is part of the diocesan community, and the diocese—the community of all of our local churches—is part of the universal Catholic Church. We are all a part of this Christian community." Rob looked around at the inquirers: new minds, new faces, new hearts to guide to the grace of God. He loved leading RCIA, loved to look around the congregation at Mass and see his surrogate children, such as they were, successive generations of Catholics he had nurtured. He felt an exhilaration pass through him, a shiver of anticipation, like an expectant father awaiting the birth of his child.

"Why don't we each take a moment to tell a bit about ourselves, and why we're here?" The group murmured with nervous laughter, shifting in seats, then silence.

"I'll start," he said. "My name is Rob Souza. I'm the pastor here at St. Justin Martyr. I was the associate pastor before Monsignor Finley died, and before that, I was a seminarian." He paused a moment for effect, then added, "I'm not married." The group laughed, as he had known they would. Rob looked to a young man at one end of the semicircle.

"I'm Alan," the man said, pushing at his thick glasses self-consciously. "I'm a software engineer at Data Basics. I decided to join the Church because my fiancée is Catholic, and I want to learn something about her religion before we get married and have children."

And so on, around the room. As the individuals spoke, Rob took brief notes: *already baptized, needs godparent, refer to Engaged Encounter.* "Welcome," he said again and again. "Thanks for coming."

At the far end of the semicircle sat an auburn-haired woman, arms and legs crossed, almost hunched in her chair. Rob guessed her to be about twenty-five. She spoke softly and didn't meet anyone's eyes.

"I'm Jessica Elliot. I was never baptized, and I've never belonged to any religion. I've gone to all different kinds of churches. But they never felt right to me, like something was always missing. Then I found a Catholic Church, and it felt—*good*, it felt like —." Rob waited for her to continue. Then the woman shrugged, abandoning the simile, and looked at her hands, closed in tight balls in her lap. "Anyway, here I am," she said, suddenly opening her slender hands like white flowers.

"Welcome." Again Rob felt a thrill, a delight in discovery. Here was exactly the kind of person he loved to have in RCIA: thoughtful, spiritual, with a desire to learn. Such people made the best converts. He watched her downturned face, her pale hands now folded in her lap, as if hiding something precious between them. Rob drew his gaze from her hands and focused on his note cards, the bullet points of his overview, and addressed the group.

"So here we all are. Now we know a little about one another, so we have already begun to become a community. We are a community of inquirers—*literally*. The first phase of the RCIA program is a preparation phase called 'Inquiry.' We'll have a chance to get to know each other, and to see if each of you is ready to take another step on the journey to conversion."

He looked around the room as he spoke, met people's eyes, and rested his gaze like a blessing on every head. *Come to us*, he invited silently.

"In the second phase, you become *catechumens*. A catechumen is an unbaptized person. It's a Greek word — it means 'questioning' or 'learning,' like *catechism*. If you're already baptized, we call you a candidate. You'll become catechumens or candidates at a ceremony in November."

Rob continued to explain how the RCIA program worked, down his checklist: Tuesday night meetings, Sunday morning worship, reading and prayer and questions answered until the Easter Vigil in April, when the baptisms, Confirmations, and First Communions would take place. He smiled, remembering the previous Easter, seven new Catholics at the altar, their hair still damp from the baptismal pool and their faces radiant with joy.

A hand rose. "What's the Easter Vigil?"

"The Vigil is the night before Easter Sunday. It's like saying 'Easter Eve.' It's the holiest night of the church year," explained Rob.

"Oh. I though Christmas was the big night of the year."

"A lot of people think that, but the Easter Vigil is definitely it. Just wait. You'll see," Rob promised. "After Easter, when everyone has become a full member of the Church, we continue to meet, explore the experiences we shared and to strengthen our commitment and our sense of community.

Pentecost ends the RCIA year in May." That was the last bullet point. He stacked his cards neatly again.

Rob answered a few questions, and then Harold, the music leader, strummed the first notes of a song on his guitar while a volunteer passed out song sheets. The inquirers began hesitantly, but Rob and his team sang, and soon other voices joined, strengthened, and filled the room.

Let all who thirst come to living water.
Let the hungry ones come to the Lord.

After the song, Rob led a brief prayer. The Catholics responded with hearty "Amens" and blessed themselves; the inquirers followed clumsily, a half-second behind. They'll learn, Rob thought, as people gathered their jackets and purses. He stacked his note cards on his yellow pad and laid the black pen, capped, alongside on the slant of the podium. The inviting scent of coffee wafted in from the hospitality room, and he merged with the stragglers, behind the soft-spoken Jessica, as she went toward the door. He saw her loose hair, an aureole of bronze in the yellow light, curling untamed on her shoulders. Rob touched her arm to get her attention.

"Oh—" she gasped, turned, fingers splayed, green eyes wide, before she saw the priest. She blushed.

"Sorry, I didn't mean to startle you." He gestured toward the hospitality room. "I just wanted to invite you to stay for some coffee."

"I have to get up pretty early in the morning for work." She fumbled with her purse strap, eyes down.

"Come have a quick piece of cake, then. This is the fun part." Rob smiled. "I mean, after my fascinating talk."

She gave a small smile back, and Rob held the door for her as they passed through.

A volunteer named Caroline was handing out crumbly squares of frosted marble cake on mismatched paper plates left over from various birthday and holiday parties. They stood among the chatting inquirers, Rob joining in other conversations, Jessica standing mute but observant as they ate their cake and sipped coffee. Rob laughed at someone's joke and then turned back to the silent Jessica. "Where do you work?" he asked, to draw her out.

"For a book publisher in the city."

"That sounds like a good job." He watched her as she cut the slice of cake into tiny bites. He prompted her, "What do you do, exactly?"

"I'm in acquisitions. I read proposals and make recommendations to the publisher. It's nice. It's not what I had planned to do, but I like it."

"Oh, what did you want to do instead?"

"I was going to be a teacher, but I—changed my mind." Her expression ended the line of inquiry. She looked down at her paper plate, and Rob saw how her red-gold lashes lay like silken fringe against her cheeks.

He looked away, sipping his coffee and surveying the room, glad to see the others talking with each other.

Jessica ate her last bite of cake. "I have to go now. I catch the train pretty early in the morning." She dropped her plate into the trash and turned back to him.

"Thanks for coming," Rob said. "We'll see you next week, then?" He set down his plate and cup, put out his hand, and she shook it briefly, her fingertips cool to his warm hand. Then she walked out the door, keys in hand.

"Father Rob!" He turned to more conversation, handshakes, laughter out the door until the room was empty but for Rob and Tran, another of his volunteers. They swept up and washed spoons and forks. Tran said goodnight and left. Rob went through the church building, locking all the doors and turning off lights. He kissed the smooth marble of the altar in the dim red glow of the sanctuary candle, pressed his lips to the cold stone over the hidden place where a tiny desiccated relic, a bone chip of the martyred St. Justin, lay, then paused a few moments on his knees before the great crucifix in the sanctuary, as he did every night while locking up. The great oak doors whispered behind him and closed with a soft click. He pulled hard to secure them.

Rob stood in the dark outside the doors of St. Justin and breathed the balmy air of a warm September night. Wind rustled through the pale leaves of a trio of birch trees near the church. A half-moon began its ascent in the eastern sky. He thought about his new inquirers, about Jessica, tentative, reluctant, and her pale hands bare of rings. She had revealed little to him, mere tidbits, but there emanated from her a tendril of need, an air of confused longing, not for him, but for something, some healing, perhaps; he was suffused with a desire that was almost paternal, to comfort her and guide her, to fold her into the loving arms of Church. But his feeling was almost not paternal, was nearly something else, and he crushed the image like a sheet of paper and thrust it aside, into the dark corner where the wraith of Shannon lingered.

Rob took a deep breath. It'll be a pleasure to watch her conversion, he told himself. Nothing more. He walked around the back way though the parking lot to the darkened rectory that he called home.

CHAPTER FOUR

Jessica rose and sang, knelt and prayed. Listened, recited, chanted. That was Mass. There was a rhythm to the Mass that she had grown to love, particularly on feast days, when the rituals were extended. The priest, the same Father Rob who led her RCIA class, said special prayers addressed to saints, to virgins and martyrs, and the choir sang hymns that seemed chosen especially for her. An altar boy swung the brass censer before him; scented gray smoke drifted through the holes and out into the church. Jessica breathed the fruity musk—was it frankincense and myrrh?

Some days the priest walked around the church with a silver bowl of holy water, dipped his fingers and sprinkled the congregation. People crossed themselves when the holy drops of water splashed them. Jessica copied the strangely pagan motions that brought tears to her eyes. What made the water holy, and why? She hoped the meaning of these rituals would be explained in her Tuesday evening class.

But even an ordinary Sunday like today could bring her to tears. Father Rob came up the center aisle as the congregation sang the opening hymn. From her pew she saw him pass, watched as he walked, singing, his black polished shoes peeping from beneath the colored robes he had donned for that Sunday's Mass. Today he wore green because it was Ordinary Time, the twenty-fifth Sunday.

Jessica followed the Mass in the missal, the book that contained the readings for each day, and the prayers; a parishioner had shown her where to look a few months before and now Jessica almost didn't need to follow the book. She had begun to know what to expect. She watched as the priest held his hands over the little circle of bread and the golden cup of wine, said the words that blessed them, and knew that the priest now held the Body and Blood of Jesus for the faithful.

When it was time to receive Communion, Jessica stayed in her seat, squashed herself into the corner of the pew while the Catholics stepped past her. They all seemed so sure of themselves, with the same folded hands, the same shuffle as they followed one another up the line to the front. There, they'd lift their hands; from her seat she could sometimes hear Father Rob say, "The Body of Christ." They'd *Amen* and receive the wafer, place it in their mouths. She watched with the mute wonder of a neophyte. What happened at that moment? How did it differ from a piece of bread? What made it taste like Jesus?

Jessica had never received Communion, and couldn't do so until she was baptized at Easter. For now, she was unworthy. She felt, more than saw, the sideways glances as she knelt, knew that people wondered why she didn't receive. She bowed her head and prayed, alone in her pew as the families shuffled by, as best she could.

Here I am, God. I don't know if You want me, or where You want me to go, but show me the way. Help me. Heal me.

That was all she could think of. Perhaps He heard.

CHAPTER FIVE

"To my excellent friends—thank you for joining me at the Church of the Erection!" Father Lawrence Poole raised his glass of wine as the priests laughed.

"Hear, hear!"

Their glasses clinked. Rob and the other priests had gathered for their regular Friday night dinner, this week Lawrence's place, in the Church of the Resurrection's rectory, because Father Tom Connors, Lawrence's pastor, was out of town. Not that Tom would have objected to the dinner party, but he would have wanted to join them, and Tom was, in their kindest view, a little weird; the younger priests did not miss him. Tom's absence gave Lawrence the freedom to entertain, and he had indulged himself and his friends with a pasta dinner, and a sauce he'd just discovered in Tuscany over the summer. Now all that remained of the feast was empty plates and anticipation of dessert.

Rob watched as Lawrence splashed brandy into a pan and lit it. With a whoosh, the alcohol burned off and the liquid simmered furiously. Lawrence shook the pan to blend the liquids, and then slipped sliced bananas into the pan.

"Mmm, bananas. My favorite fruit!" Father Philomel Lacaro leaned his bulk over the counter to observe. His clerical shirt was untucked and showed a pale moon of obtrusive skin at his waist.

"I thought I was your favorite fruit." Father William Fairlie draped his long arm around Phil's shoulder. Father Cesar Castro tittered behind his hand, while Father Hector Salvo sniffed his disapproval.

"Sorry, Father." Phil patted William's hand. "You'll get over me."

Hector watched Lawrence cook with a look of distaste.

"What's the matter, Hector?" Lawrence asked, winking at his guests. "Indigestion?" Hector had eaten his pasta plain, his salad without dressing, and refused the wine. His hypochondria was legendary, and his delicate constitution a target of regular teasing.

"No. I can't eat bananas. They make my mouth itch."

The boys hooted and clapped him on the shoulder. "I'll bet they do!" Hector sniffed and turned away.

Lawrence spooned out the dessert while Rob put forks on the plates and handed them to the priests. They left the kitchen and sat down in the living room.

William tasted his dessert. "Mmm, I love big slippery bananas," he said with a lingering look at Hector.

"We've heard," Rob said. "More than we want to know." He set his wine glass on the coffee table. "This is excellent, Lawrence. Are we celebrating already?"

"Oh, yes. I've finished scoring the entrance antiphon of my Mass." Lawrence hummed a few notes. "The last few days have been delicious, with Tom out of town. The Muse, she has been most cooperative." Lawrence closed his eyes, as if hearing music in his mind.

"You've had to cover all the Masses, though." Cesar blew delicately on the warm dessert. "*And* the sick calls, *and* the confessions, everything."

"Yeah, but still, I love having this place to myself."

"Uh-oh—he's having delusions of grandeur. He thinks he's pastor now," Phil teased.

"Hardly! But I've accomplished so much these past few days. I just wish I had more quiet time before Tom gets home." Lawrence closed his eyes again, humming softly.

"Oh, you miss him, don't lie!"

Lawrence opened his eyes and made a face. "Oh, yeah, like I really missed his meditation music and herbal tea and pyramid power. Groovy, man." Lawrence flashed peace signs at his friends. "No, seriously, we get along all right. He doesn't bother me most of the time. But I savor the silence when he's gone."

Cesar set down his plate and wiped his fingers with great care. He folded his cloth napkin neatly and laid it next to his plate, then looked up and saw the others watching him. "What?"

"C'mon, Cesar. Don't hold back." William nudged him.

Cesar worked in the Office of Worship and always heard gossip first. He might rush to tell, or he might wait, smug and superior, until someone teased it out of him. One of his nicknames was Gladys Kravitz, after the nosy neighbor on *Bewitched*.

"You *know* something, Sleazer." Lawrence grinned. "It's so obvious!"

"Well!" Cesar folded his arms across his chest and looked primly at his peers.

"Rob, what shall we do with him?" Lawrence asked.

"Oh, make him wash the dishes, to start," Rob suggested.

"What, and get dishpan hands?"

"If you must know." Cesar took a deep breath and looked at Lawrence. "I heard something about *you*."

"What about me?"

"Well, something that affects you. Since you'll be working so hard on this musical project, Tom was asking if he could get some additional help. He requested an associate. And he got one. I saw the paperwork."

"*I'm* the associate pastor. He doesn't need another one."

"Not another associate pastor, a *pastoral associate*. An assistant."

"Here it comes," Rob said. "Who is it, Sleazer?"

Cesar paused dramatically. "A nun."

"Noooo!" Phil and William groaned loudly.

Lawrence shrugged. "I don't mind a nun, if it'll free me to write the music."

"Who is it?" Rob asked again.

"Sister Therese Fallon." He pronounced the name *Trayz*.

William hooted. "Oh, my God! Pack your bags, Lorenzo, your days are numbered." He laughed into his hands until he coughed. "Oh, dear!"

Rob and Phil shook their heads at each other. "Never heard of her," Rob said to Lawrence. "Do you know her?"

Lawrence shrugged. "Nope."

"Well, you will." William coughed again, struggling to compose himself. "She's a total control freak. She was with Jim Pollock at All Saints, remember? And he fired her, or got her moved somehow. She drove him nuts, followed him around, and mucked up everything. Then she left the diocese for a while, went up the North Coast to commune with otters or worship whales or some kind of woman-warrior shit. She sounds like a perfect match for Tom. And now she's back!"

Lawrence looked at Rob with dread. "Dear Lord."

William wiped his eyes. "Oh, my God, Lawrence. I pity you, I really do."

CHAPTER SIX

Autumn was the season Jessica dreaded most. She kept her sweater wrapped around her, her wild hair battened down in a braid or twisted into a knot. She wore gloves when it was cold, scarves and hats on gusty days, long sleeves, full skirts, dark colors, bulky knits, anything to keep the eyes at bay, to guard what remained from what had been thrust into her and carved out of her. So girded, she kept busy enough to not remember.

She didn't read the newspapers or watch the news, only played classical music, wordless, unobtrusive, on her radio, and she turned down the sound when the news came on. There was always another story of assault and battery, molestation, a serial rapist on the loose, someone else's life destroyed or soiled beyond redemption. Swaying on the train to work in the mornings, she averted her eyes, or kept them focused in her book to avoid the headlines in nearby papers. On the way home again, as the cool day darkened early into night, it was the same, nose in the book, hunched in the corner of the seat if she got one, her feet pressing the floor as if to gas the train along, hurry her home.

Saturdays reprieved her, when she didn't have to work, when she could stay home and nest. Jessica stood at the stove, hot jam bubbling in her grandma's old yellow kettle, jam jars simmering sterile in the boiler, the apron another comfortable layer around her waist. The sieved blackberries foamed in the kettle like ebony lava, and emitted puffs of fruity steam. She stood at arm's length to stir, but sometimes the slurry spat, caught her wrist and burned a molten sugar brand. Jessica held the red wrist, a penance, under cold water.

When the jam had cooked long enough, she ladled it into clear jars, tapped the vacuum lids on and left them to set. Later, she added the half-pints to her open shelves, already laden with jars. Plum jam glowed ruby next to golden peaches suspended in syrup the color of sunrise; translucent green slices of cucumber in their herbs and salty brine adjacent to the caramel spice of applesauce. She'd picked and gathered all the fruit at her parents' country home, two hours away, where she spent her summer weekends, weeding, culling, helping her mother to preserve, and bringing home bags and bowls of fruit to can at home. Everything but the pears, bald and white, like bloated fetuses bobbing in jars.

The women had worked in the garden, side by side, and then stood at the sink, rinsed gray dust from the fruit, baked and canned, hours with her mother, her sister, never once talking of anything real, as if under a vow of silence. The Sonoma landscape became her Eden, where if she wouldn't talk about it, it didn't exist, and she was still as serene as if she had never left.

Jessica hung her apron on a hook and went outside to check the mail. The sun had broken through the long morning overcast, and now she felt its thin warmth on her face. She sat outside on the apartment steps in crisp autumn air and breathed the scent of damp leaves, watched her shadow fade and sharpen as a cloud passed over the sun. As days grew short, the sun weakened as if dying, and there were days on which she hardly cast a shadow, and began to wonder if she were still visible, or if she had finally faded altogether, evaporated from the world.

Another cloud smudged the light, and she gave up on sun warmth. Jessica went inside and turned on the heater, took up her needlepoint, and curled in a chair with her cat nearby. Around her, the small apartment displayed her handiwork: hand-stitched quilts that covered her bed, nubby afghans draped across the sofa, a cascade of needlepoint pillows, stacks of embroidered tea towels in the kitchen. Hours otherwise empty filled with busy-work, layers of fabrics and batting, thread and needle, a soft cocoon that she built, stitch by stitch, to keep her safe.

CHAPTER SEVEN

Rob was working at the computer when the doorbell rang, then the door opened with its usual creak.

"Anybody home?"

"Back here," Rob called. He came out of the office into the hall and grinned when he saw his friend Father Patrick Keegan, the young pastor at Queen of Heaven. "Hey, there!" Rob greeted him with a hug.

"Hey. I was just passing by and thought I'd drop in, say hi." Patrick stuck his hands into his pockets. "Want to go grab some lunch?"

"I'd love to, but I'm trying to finish this handout for RCIA, then I have to go over to the convent at 2 o'clock. How about I make us a sandwich here?"

Patrick shrugged, not his usually talkative self.

Rob led the way into the rectory kitchen and began pulling lettuce, cheese, and condiments from the refrigerator. He found himself chattering to fill the strained silence. "Is turkey all right? I think I have some ham in there, too."

"Whatever."

"You like mustard?"

"Sure."

"How about a soda? I've got some in the fridge. Help yourself."

"Thanks," Patrick said, but he didn't open the refrigerator. Instead, he leaned against the counter with his arms folded tightly against his dark woolen sweater and watched Rob work.

"Rob."

"Hmm?" Rob looked up from his sandwiches.

Patrick's clear gray eyes were full of tears.

"What, Patrick? What's going on?" Rob set the knife down.

Patrick took a breath. "It's Katie." He wiped a shaking hand across his eyes. "She's pregnant."

"My God, Patrick. Your baby?"

"Yes, my baby."

"I thought you were going to end that. You said you were breaking up with her." Rob had learned of the affair when Patrick made his confession, but they had not spoken of it since.

"Well I didn't, obviously."

"I guess not," Rob said, a little too forcefully. "I'm sorry. I'm not judging you. But what are you going to do? Is she going to have it? She's not —."

"No, no, never that. She's going to keep it. God, Rob, I'm scared shitless. What if this gets out? If there's publicity? What about my parish? The Bishop? Shit!"

"Never mind the other stuff," Rob said. "What about Kate?"

"That's the one good thing." Patrick wiped his eyes again. "She's so happy. She really wants to have this baby. But it's not like I can marry her. I'll have to find some way to support her. I can't feed a kid with what I make. I can barely make my car payment now." Patrick massaged his pale brow. "Damn it!"

"When's she due?"

"Next month."

"Patrick!" Rob tried to keep his voice low, but he was furious. "For God's sake! What are you thinking?"

"She was afraid I'd want her to have an abortion—which I would never ask. I don't want that. I want her to have my baby. But I'm a priest. Rob, I've only been ordained two years. I don't know what to do. I just feel like—like I'm paralyzed. I can't breathe. I should be with Katie, totally happy, and I'm just sick to death." He rubbed his forehead again, and ran fingers through his fine black hair.

"Well, you can't just do nothing. You're going to have to tell the Bishop, or someone else'll find out and tell him first. And *someone* will tell him, you know."

"I can't. I just don't know. Maybe we can keep it quiet for a while, just wait and see what happens." Patrick's gray eyes met Rob's.

"That's not fair to Kate. You know that."

"It's the only thing I can think of to do. Just for a while. Don't tell anyone, okay?"

"Don't do this." Rob held up a hand. "Don't put me in this position. Don't do this to Kate. And don't do it to yourself. Please—do the right thing."

"Fine. Fine." Patrick looked away. "Just tell me—what's the right thing to do?"

The two priests faced each other across the tiled counter.

A baby. A woman. A wife.

"I don't know."

Advent

CHAPTER EIGHT

"What do you ask of God's Church?" Father Rob's voice resonated through the church.

"Everlasting life."

"What do you ask of God's Church?"

"True faith."

What indeed? Jessica stood in line, trembling, waiting for her turn to respond. It was the first Sunday of Advent, cold rain and wind outside. The time had come for the RCIA group to make the first official step toward joining the Catholic Church. Inside, on that stormy morning, the parish of St. Justin Martyr was celebrating the Rite of Acceptance into the Order of Catechumens.

The RCIA group was gathered in the vestibule. They were not to enter the sanctuary of church that day until they had been ritually welcomed in. Each of the members was partnered with a sponsor or a godparent now. Jessica stood beside Susan, her future godparent, a married woman of a similar age, and listened to the opening of the Mass. Father Rob's voice carried from the front of the church out the double doors to the vestibule. Jessica's legs kept shaking.

"All those eyes, Susan. I can't stand everyone looking at me." She shivered as if someone had trailed cold fingers down her spine.

"Don't worry," Susan comforted. "Just keep your eyes on Father Rob. Nothing else will matter."

"Let us go out to meet them," Father Rob's voice announced.

A wave of nervous nausea rolled through Jessica. The parishioners herded slowly out from their pews toward the large vestibule, surrounding the ten RCIA members and their sponsors. Jessica looked at the grout between the brown tiles on the floor.

Father Rob, majestic in his violet Advent chasuble, stopped in front of the line of newcomers and greeted them, "Welcome, friends."

His voice reached her, and she lifted her gaze up to his. He smiled at them, at her, and she felt heartened. Like she might be strong enough to say it when the time came. Strong enough to tell.

Jessica had quit her teaching career before it even started. No one, not her roommates, not her parents, could understand why she ditched everything she had studied for. She had liked living in San Francisco, sharing an apartment with two friends. She worked as a sales clerk in a bookstore on weekends, met friends for coffee, and sometimes dated other teaching students. She worked hard and got good grades in her classes.

In the fall of her final year, she began work on her senior project, a study of children in a local preschool. A fellow student offered to partner her in the project, and she agreed. One night he showed up at her apartment, beer on his breath. He came on to her, tried to kiss her, wouldn't take no for an answer. Jessica bolted for the door, but he grabbed at her, caught her thick bronzy hair in his tight fist, and pulled her to him, and down.

Her throat seemed clenched. No screams would come out. No way to pull away. He held her face to the wiry carpet and ripped, tore, pushed, thrust, emptied into her, collapsed, crushing her into the dank wool of the rug.

She lay, shaking, her face on the floor, as he rolled away. He left her there, tangled hair and open blouse, an arc of buttons sprayed across the carpet, her skirt ripped away. She crouched on the floor like an animal, clutching her rags, wracked with sobs, until she thought of her roommates, and when they might be home.

They can't see me like this. No one can know.

Jessica stood up shakily. Her throat felt raw, her scalp sore from yanked hair, her insides torn with every move. She went into the bathroom and took off the rest of her clothes. She turned on the shower, scalding heat, and stared at herself in the mirror, wild halo of hair, red-rimmed eyes like a rabbit, until steam filmed the glass.

How could she have been so stupid? Why couldn't she have seen? What message had she given? What could she have done? No answer was right.

Jessica dropped the class. She struggled to finish the school year. She graduated without pomp or circumstance in June and moved to a small studio elsewhere in the City. Then away from the City altogether.

Stupid.

She needed a ritual cleansing, a state of grace. A way to go on and forgive herself for letting it happen. A way to forget. She walked into one church, then another, found empty walls, antiseptic ministers. They knew nothing of her need, of the void she felt. She couldn't pray to an empty cross, with a minister who looked like a suit from the Financial District. There was no Jesus there.

One summer day, for lack of a better plan, she walked the side streets of the historic district of her town, wandering and looking. Those restored Victorian and Queen Anne houses were the town's glory, but she felt nothing for them. The sun blazed hot on her neck. Dazzled by the heat and light, she climbed pink steps into a church. Inside was cool and dark and the people prayed on their knees. The marble statues gazed in sorrowful silence. In one glance Jessica knew that they understood penance and suffering. Even Jesus, bloody suffering Jesus, wore a crown of thorns.

She walked quietly around the margin of the church, pausing to look at the icons, the flickering votives, to hear the click of beads. She took a leaflet and read the words *confession* and *absolution.* Virgins and martyrs everywhere. A church that honored even Mary Magdalene, a prostitute, couldn't reject her, could become her spiritual home. She sank to her knees to pray.

"What do you ask of God's Church?" Father Rob looked at her, his eyes unpiercing, kind.

"The peace of Christ," she whispered. "Amen."

CHAPTER NINE

Fathers Cesar Castro and Phil Lacaro had already ordered when Rob finally arrived at the restaurant. Raindrops glistened in his dark hair, and his jacket was spotted with drops. "Sorry I'm late. What did I miss?"

"Not much," said Phil as Rob took his seat.

"Just Phil's dinner order," added Cesar. "The kitchen staff almost fainted when it went in."

The pungent scent of sesame oil filled the air as a young Asian waiter passed, bearing a platter of steaming noodles; his sleeves were rolled provocatively high on golden, muscled arms. Phil inhaled deeply, his eyes rolled back in ecstasy. "Oh, I want some of that."

Cesar sipped his tea. "So get some."

The Chinese restaurant was full this evening, and noisy. The room was long and narrow, with small square tables arranged along both walls, and a few larger round tables in the center. The walls were painted a pale pink and hung with delicate brush paintings of bridges, herons, and misty mountains.

A waitress came to the table, whipping her pad from her apron pocket. Her hair was twisted in a tight French knot, her heels too high for quick movement. She tapped her pen on the pad impatiently and gave Rob an exasperated look. "Ready to order?"

He saw her fingers, long and slender, with fuchsia talons that gleamed in the light. "The Szechwan chicken dinner, please."

"You want a separate check?" Her dark eyes dared him to ask.

"No, no, just add it to the other."

She tapped sharply away.

"She's charming, isn't she?" Phil commented.

"Not terribly." Cesar dismissed her.

"Where's Hector?" Rob looked around for their friend. "Couldn't he make it?"

"Oh, he's home at the rectory," Cesar answered. "He's ill."

"Or thinks he is," added Phil. He pointed at his head and made curlicues with his finger.

"Poor Hector." Rob chuckled. "Someday he really will be sick, and no one will believe him."

The waitress returned to the table with Phil's appetizers. Delicate tendrils of steam wafted upwards from golden spring rolls. The chicken wings lay in a nutty brown sauce, sprinkled with sesame seeds. The other priests watched him eat with morbid fascination.

Then Cesar remembered. "Ooh, have you heard? Lawrence's nun has arrived."

Phil stopped eating. "Noooo! Sister Therese? When?"

"Last week, I think. Lawrence is in despair already. He can't stand her. It's giving him dropsy or something."

"So she's torturing our boy?"

"Apparently." Lawrence had been calling morning and night since the arrival of Therese. "She's fiddling with his files and giving priestly advice on the phone. Lawrence says she thinks *she's* the priest."

"Maybe she became a Protty on her retreat," Phil cracked.

"No, I don't think so," Rob said, chuckling. "She came back from her sabbatical with a bunch of brilliant ideas for improving the liturgy. Poor Lawrence."

The waitress arrived with Rob's dinner. She set the plate down, slapped the bill in the center of the table, and whirled briskly back to the kitchen.

"*Bon appétit.*" Phil grinned at Rob.

Cesar watched Rob eat. "I heard something else." He spoke casually, as if it wasn't important at all.

"Like what?"

"Something about someone we all know and love."

Phil stopped eating and rested his chin on his meaty fist. "Tell us everything."

"Patrick—" Cesar stopped as Rob glanced up, a hard look on his face.

"Keegan?" Phil belched into his hand. "What about him?"

Cesar looked at Rob. "He's a father."

"A Father?" Phil brightened. "Ooh, you mean a daddy! Does the Bishop know?"

"I don't think so."

"Who told you?" Rob asked.

"William. He went by Queen of Heaven to borrow Patrick's Spanish Lectionary. And there was a girl there with Patrick, with a newborn baby. William thought it was an appointment for a baptism, until he saw the baby. It looks just like Patrick, he said." Cesar sipped his tea, avoiding Rob's eyes.

"Give me a break," Phil scoffed. "Babies all look the same—like smashed pumpkins."

"No, that's what I said. But William said it has the same eyes, same dark hair."

"So that makes it his baby?"

"I don't know. I wasn't there." Cesar's round cheeks reddened. A whine edged his voice. "William said. He said it was that girl that Patrick liked, and the baby looked just like him, and the girl was all clingy and wifey."

"Cesar, do us a favor and don't spread this around." Rob spoke softly. "You know what'll happen if the Bishop finds out. Or the newspapers or the TV stations, for God's sake. It's not only Patrick. It's all of us." Rob tapped his fingers sharply on the table, thinking. "Whether we're guilty or innocent—just like last time."

The year before, one of the priests had gotten a teenage girl pregnant. As soon as a parishioner heard rumors, she had run to the newspapers. Never mind that the facts were mortifying enough. The priest had been sent off to the clergy rehabilitation center in New Mexico and a hefty settlement made to the teen and her family; the entire phalanx of priests had been hounded by the media for months. And ongoing priestly scandals elsewhere hadn't helped the Church's reputation.

Cesar raised his palms, swearing, "It stops here. I won't breathe a word to anyone else." He actually looked like he meant it. "Let's change the subject, shall we?"

Rob drank his tea. He gave Cesar a smile, and saw Cesar relax. *Poor Sleazer. I shouldn't have jumped all over him. It's not his fault.* But if the Bishop didn't know about Patrick by now, it was only a matter of time.

CHAPTER TEN

The chords came to him. "*Gloria,*" Lawrence sang. Down a third. No. Up again. *No.* He moved up a seventh. "Glory to God in the Highest. *Gloria.*" Better. Still not right, though. It wanted more reverence, passion, joy. He played an augmented fourth, the so-called Devil's Interlude, for a darker tone. Oh, that was better still. And the irony did not escape him.

The *Gloria* was a hymn of celebration to God for all His blessings. Lawrence repeated the interlude, still not satisfied. He flexed his hands and wiggled his fingers to limber them. He played a bit that had run through his head last night as he'd drifted to sleep, a hint of what might come. And suddenly it came, in a rush, the right notes. He heard it, had it all. He played it twice, a quick riff just to remember it.

Lawrence had been hard at work on his opus for the recording contract when the call came. The Bishop himself asked Lawrence, at utterly the worst time and at absolutely the last minute, to write a piece of music for the Christmas Mass at the cathedral. Lawrence had a scant two weeks until Christmas, and he had to finish the Bishop's *Gloria*, print and copy it, distribute it to the cathedral choir, rehearse and perfect it—or whatever passed for perfection with the cathedral's choir—by Christmas Eve. Fortunately, with just a bit of tweaking, Lawrence could probably use the same *Gloria* for the CD. But that didn't make the work any less stressful.

Humming the notes under his breath, Lawrence erased his penciled notes and rewrote them on the scribbled score sheet. There was a hint of the sublime there. Smiling, he played again what he had written. "Glory to God in—"

But something distracted him, something moved at the corner of his vision. He swiveled on the piano bench, just catching sight of Resurrection's new associate, Sister Therese, as she crossed his private patio, her favorite shortcut to the rectory. He heard her come into the rectory, slam the door, and burst into her own office, keys jangling, files dropping to her desk. Then she committed what was, to Lawrence, the ultimate sin. She turned on her radio to an oldies station. Loudly.

The elusive music evaporated.

Lawrence threw down his pencil, thrust back the piano bench and headed for the door. She *knew* he was working. She *knew* he had a deadline. At the door, he stopped. *Take a deep breath. Don't go in there like a psychopath.* He took a controlled breath, opened the door, and walked up the hall.

Sister Therese Fallon, twig-thin and wiry with energy, sat at her desk, sorting files and singing with the radio, "You ain't nothin' but a hound dawg..." Her salt-and-pepper hair was cut close to her head like a cap, and her small stature gave her an elfin look.

"Oh, hello there, Father." Her voice was honeyed. "And what can I do for you today?" A commercial for a monster truck rally roared through the radio's speaker.

"Would you mind turning off the radio? I'm trying to finish the *Gloria* for Christmas." He gave her a tight smile.

"Oh, I'll just turn it down a notch. Then it won't bother you." Therese reached over to her bookcase and turned the volume down one tiny notch. She looked up at Lawrence with green-gold eyes. "That good enough?" A cola commercial began, raucous and jarring.

"I'm afraid not." His pulse pounded hard in his ears. "Therese, your office is so close that every sound you make comes right through the walls. I have a deadline for the Bishop that I must meet. I simply can't work with your radio on. Would you mind, please, turning it off?" There, Lawrence thought, that was polite yet firm, and he had invoked the Bishop as well, for extra leverage.

"Well, Father," Therese emphasized his formal title. "I find it disturbing to work with *your* music playing. I need my radio to drown out all that noise. So if I turn it off, you'll be disturbing *me*. And then I can't work. And then Father Tom will be so disappointed in both of us. So either you play or I work. And, with all due respect, I have a lot of work to do, so perhaps you can play later." She smiled at him, her cat eyes narrowed, and pointedly bent to her work.

Lawrence turned and walked out. He went into the music room and closed the door, leaning against it, shaking with unspent anger. That *woman*. He couldn't work; he couldn't compose anything with her in the rectory. He wished with all his heart that his pastor, Father Tom Connors, had never hired Therese.

Therese, a nun of many talents, had taken seminars in popular ministry, practiced liturgical miming and modern dance, and considered herself gifted at interpreting the Sacred Scriptures through movement. It was *her art*, she told parishioners.

Lawrence could almost forgive Therese's artistic endeavors, but for her influence on their pastor. Their styles were maddeningly alike, which was to say, in direct opposition to anything that Lawrence might suggest or prefer.

Lawrence knew his pastor, Tom, had a good heart. But Lawrence was a student of classic Catholicism, looking to the Early Church for direction in liturgy, while Tom's views had left him steadfastly in the 1970s where modern worship was concerned. When only the two priests had shared the parish, they'd been able to balance their opposite styles. But when Therese arrived, Lawrence was out of the loop; suddenly Therese and Tom had the only opinions that mattered.

"You know, the reason we have priests is because we need someone to lead the liturgy," Lawrence contended at the first liturgy committee meeting. "If we rule by committee, nothing gets done. Sometimes we just have to make an executive decision for the good of the parish."

"But we must include everyone," Therese insisted. The next week she set up a slide projector before Mass, and during the songs, she showed her own slides of ladybugs on rose petals, children playing on the beach, and of course, clowns. Worse, in Lawrence's eyes, she introduced secular music and readings. Instead of a quiet meditation period after Communion, Therese read from the *Desiderata* or the Alcoholics Anonymous *Big Book*. She had actually read her own post-modern-feminist poetry on a recent Sunday. Lawrence cringed, remembering. There were some lines that just shouldn't be crossed.

"We have to make people feel comfortable here," Therese said at the staff meeting. "We have to hold their interest." As if the congregation was a paying audience, as if they wouldn't come to worship without her clever ideas. Lawrence, who was a trained musician, for God's sake, took great care to plan the music for Mass, but Therese, bypassing Lawrence's plans, instructed the pianist to play theme songs from popular children's movies during Family Liturgy and the school Masses, because, "It makes the kids feel included."

"That should fill the pews," Tom gloated to Lawrence over dinner.

"But that isn't good liturgy," Lawrence tried to reason with Tom. "It's a God-and-pony show. You can't keep subverting the order of worship. People don't come here for the Ringling Brothers version of Jesus. What's next? We'll all be wearing love beads and singing 'One Tin Soldier' and rolling naked in body paint, for God's sake. It's crap-worship and you know it!"

"Lawrence, I'm sensing some hostility here," Tom said. "Perhaps you should explore why you're so resistant to an empowering liturgy." He sipped his wheat grass juice.

Lawrence wholeheartedly believed in Church, in creating liturgy that was spiritual rather than mere entertainment, and he despised the cute themes, the sloppy, haphazard liturgy that Therese devised and Tom rubber-stamped during endless liturgy committee meetings.

Lawrence couldn't make them see. He couldn't make Therese go away, and he couldn't bring Tom out of his groovier reality. Lawrence withdrew from the liturgy committee, which would bow to Tom and Therese anyway. He said his two Masses on Sundays; he took his turn at the daily Mass, and tried to focus on his music.

But now, thanks to Therese, even that was impossible. The rectory was meant to be the priests' residence, but Tom had given Therese office space there. Now Lawrence couldn't leave his rooms in his bathrobe to fetch a cup of coffee, nor relax in the living room with guests. He certainly couldn't sunbathe, not with Therese's habit of cutting through his private patio or showing up at all hours to work on the computer. Her radio was constantly on. The situation was beyond maddening.

Lawrence couldn't live like this. He just couldn't. He had to do something. He went through the door to his bedroom and grabbed shorts and sweats from bureau drawers, threw them into a sports bag and drove across town to the gym. He changed in the locker room and went in to use the stair machine. He got going and really pumped up the steps, his legs like pistons, climbing upward, out of the funk, up to whatever plane he could reach, high enough to hear the music again. And just as he could hear the strains of what might become a decent *Acclamation*, in the mirror, a pair of angelic brown eyes caught his.

"Hey." The angel on the next stair-machine smiled. "My name's Gabriel. What's yours?"

CHAPTER ELEVEN

Jessica sat in the armchair in her apartment, stitching. A lamp at her shoulder illuminated her work. The woolen yarn slipped easily through the mesh, black stitch by green stitch, slanting blue across the sky, gray for shadows. Beside her, from the speakers, a Gregorian chant rose and fell. In the kitchen, the faucet dripped. Her gray cat slept curled on the couch, oblivious to the winter rainstorm outside.

Jessica bowed her head to her work, glancing to follow the master chart, filling in color and pattern, over and over, one smooth motion at a time. A quick jab of the point, a thrust into the web, a jerk from behind, her arm outstretched to reveal its creamy underside. Her eyes followed the strand of thread; her arm made a graceful journey away and back. The monotony of the act lulled her. Her mind drifted.

Her face still felt imprinted from the rough carpet. Her arms might still bear the four-fingered marks, the purple that faded to the yellow-green, hidden under long sleeves on a cold day. She was always cold.

She couldn't bear the warm embrace of friends, could not abide the touch of skin on skin. She startled like a rabbit, jolted with fear when tapped from behind. The world beyond her line of sight was terrifying, beyond her control. She stood against the walls at parties, in elevators, the slight press of her shoulders against solid wall for safety. And sometimes, a certain kind of man would pass her on the street or catch her eye, enough like *him* to send her scuttling to the side and quickly away.

Her only visit to a doctor ended shamefully; clad in the humiliating paper gown, Jessica startled when he walked into the room. The doctor smiled politely, but she saw *him* in those blue eyes, heard *him* in the suggestion that she lie back. She tried not to mind, pretended she was calm, but jumped when she felt his gloved hand on her leg, and began to sob. *So stupid.* The doctor stopped immediately, was kinder than she deserved. He gave her a referral to a woman doctor and a therapist. Jessica slipped from the office in shame, business cards crushed in her pocket.

The music ended and the air was still. The faucet dripped; her kitchen clock ticked. Cars passed on the dark street. Her apartment huddled around her, shielding her from eyes and hands, from voices behind her. The needle swooped through the mesh like a diving bird.

The Holy Spirit descended on Jesus like a dove, on his disciples as raging tongues of fire. At the meetings at St. Justin Martyr on Tuesdays, the catechumens listened to Father Rob and his team of volunteers describe the Commandments, the Beatitudes, the coming of the Holy Spirit. Later, the group asked questions, described their Journey to faith, and shared their Call.

"I once heard the story of a man who looked back on his life and saw footprints in the sand. But at the most difficult times in his life, he saw only one set of footprints," a woman said.

Jessica listened from her chair in the circle, irritated beyond words by the saccharine story.

"Because the Lord carried him at the worst times in his life," the woman said. "I find so much comfort in that. The Lord carries me when I'm weak."

Jessica raised her hand. Father Rob called her name. "I've heard that story, too," she said. "I know what it's trying to say. But I just don't buy it. Life just doesn't work that way. Instead of someone carrying me at the worst times in my life, I feel like I've been dragged." Her throat thickened as if silted with sand. "I've never felt that —."

The others shifted in their chairs. Father Rob looked at her a long moment. The silence grew. Her cheeks flamed.

"If you've come here looking for easy answers, you've come to the wrong place," he said. "There's no way to refute that. You feel what you feel."

Her throat ached. She tried to swallow.

Father Rob addressed the group. "What do we do with our pain? Remember that God gave us the gift of free will; we can choose to insulate ourselves against pain and suffering, against all emotion, or we can choose to move through it, and grow from it. Believe it or not, suffering can awaken deep compassion. It can be utterly transforming. That's the message of the Resurrection. I don't mean that we want to suffer. But let's face it; bad things happen. Only you can transform the suffering in your life."

He looked back to Jessica. "Pray. Grow your faith. Move through the darkness and rise again."

In her apartment, the heater hummed to life, faintly clicking as it purred warm air into the room. Her cat yawned and stretched, looked at her with sleepy eyes. Toward the end of the row, the yarn knotted. Jessica plucked gently, unable to untangle the strand. She snipped it off at last, and began again.

Christmas

CHAPTER TWELVE

Early on Christmas Eve at the rectory of St. Cecile, where Cesar lived, the phone rang. Monsignor Grimmley, Cesar's pastor, put down his needlepoint, a golden *fleur-de-lis* against a midnight blue background meant to cover a footstool. The many shades of gold were nearly impossible to tell apart, and the tiny symbols on the chart were giving Monsignor a headache. He pushed his glasses up his nose.

Goddamn phone. "Caesar! Caesar! Answer the phone!" Where was that boy? No answer, of course. Probably out gallivanting around, the little fruitcake.

He heaved himself out of his favorite armchair and shuffled to the hallway to stop the shrill ringing. People ought to know it was too late to call. What was it, seven o'clock already? The phone rang again and again as he shambled up the hall.

"Hello, hello! St. Cecile's."

"Uh, yes, I want to know, what time is Mass on Christmas Eve?" The woman's voice squawked through the phone.

"It was listed in the Sunday bulletin last week. Didn't you get one?"

"Uh, I didn't get one last week."

Oh, for crissakes. "Weren't you at Mass on Sunday?" He knew what she would say.

"Uh, no, well, actually, we wanted to come for Christmas Eve, and I just need to know what time the Mass starts."

"Where do you live?"

"What? Oh, here in town. Is it a midnight Mass or —?"

"*Where* in town? What's your address?"

"Solano Boulevard. I just—"

"No, no," he growled. Grimmley shivered as a draft blew up the hall. *Goddamn it.* He made his voice calm and sweet. "Go look outside the front door, dear. There's a number outside on the front of your house. What is it?"

The woman hesitated. "6124 Solano."

"6124? 6124?" Where was that?

"Yeah."

"Is that the east side or west?"

"Uh, west, I guess."

Ah, now he had her. "That's St. Alphonse parish, not St. Cecile."

"Well, we just want to come to the midnight Mass—"

Monsignor hung up the phone. *Goddamn parish-hoppers.* Twice-a-year-Catholics, Christmas and Easter. He could set his goddamn watch by them. He shook his head and shuffled back to his warm chair near the television. *Wheel of Fortune* was on in ten minutes.

On Christmas Eve at St. Justin Martyr, the sanctuary was bedecked in evergreen, with simple white lights strung through trees and garlands. Their sharp tang scented the air. Red bows hung from every wreath. The choir sang softly before Mass, quiet carols of snow and shepherds, the hush before the angels came. Father Rob Souza stood in the vestibule near the burbling splash of the baptismal pool, dressed, for once, in his formal black cassock. He hugged and kissed and shook hands with his parishioners as they arrived for midnight Mass. When the clock ticked toward midnight, he stepped into the sacristy and donned his white vestments for Mass.

At the Church of the Resurrection, Father Lawrence Poole vested himself in the sacristy, silently adjusted the white chasuble and settled his white stole around his shoulders. Tonight, one of the holiest nights of the Church year, his *Gloria* would be played at the cathedral for the first time, for the Bishop and honored guests, including the city's mayor, several county supervisors and the local congressman. But tonight he must be here at Resurrection, instead of performing the debut of his *Gloria*, because Father Tom and Sister Therese said he couldn't be spared. He looked at himself in the mirror of the sacristy and straightened the vestments in silence.

At St. Ambrose, Father Philip Lacaro slept. His Christmas Eve Mass had taken place at eight o'clock, and was long over. He rolled over in his sleep and dreamed that hands caressed him. Small hands.

At St. Rita, the church was brilliantly decorated with brightly colored streamers, candles, Mexican tissue-paper snowflakes, painted wooden ornaments from El Salvador, straw angels woven in Guatemala. A mariachi band played outside the church before the Mass began. The church filled; dozens of people crowded in the back and around the sides. The procession into the church included several children, who reenacted the traditional Mexican *posada*, Mary and Joseph's search for shelter. Every parishioner seemed to be sneezing, coughing, itching, or blowing his nose.

After he had greeted far too many germ-carrying parishioners, Father Hector Salvo stepped into the sacristy to wash his hands again. Then again. His throat hurt already. At precisely midnight, he began the Mass in Spanish. "*En el nombre del Padre, y del Hijo, y del Espiritu Santo,*" he said, facing the huge germy assembly.

"*Amen,*" they responded.

At Holy Trinity Cathedral, while Lawrence Poole's haunting *Gloria* rang in the solemnity of the Mass, Bishop Paul Cornelius stood before the presider's chair and listened to the joyous notes.

At Resurrection, despite Lawrence's pleas against it beforehand, the slide show began. Therese stood in back and watched her two minions click the buttons on their respective slide projectors, which cast images of

Christmas past and present upon two screens. Parishioners sang along to the buoyant strains of *Joy to the World*, their eyes reflecting the images of sleds in snow, holly wreaths, and mounds of presents beneath a glittering Christmas tree.

Altar boys entered, carrying the processional cross; heads turned to watch the procession. Children entered behind them, dressed in Nativity-play costumes—angel wings, shepherds' rags, a blue drape for Mary. Behind them a boy dragged a real pygmy goat. It balked and bleated loudly in terror. The children reached the front of the church and stepped into position in the living crèche.

The goat jerked the young boy's arm as the child struggled to restrain him. It bellowed in its hoarse goat voice and let out a stream of raisin-like turds that bounced on the red carpet. A parent hurriedly swept up the trail. When the goat was finally maneuvered into the crèche, it began to eat the straw. Parents *ahhed*. And last came someone dressed as Santa Claus, who walked slowly up the aisle, knelt before the crèche, and crossed himself reverently. From the back of the church, Therese smiled her triumph at Lawrence.

At Queen of Heaven, Father Patrick Keegan's homily was disturbed by a baby wailing out in the congregation. He paused and said, "We are all blessed with the presence of a newborn child on this holy night of Christmas Eve!" He smiled at the baby's mother, who sat by herself in the back of the church.

At St. Perpetua, Father William Fairlie led the congregation in the Prayer of the Faithful. In his prayerful pose, he was able to see the artistically-hung holly and ivy swags around the church, the wreath of Scotch pine that encircled the purple and rose Advent candles, and the gold origami doves that bedecked the twin fir trees at either side of the sanctuary. Everything was in its place. All tastefully arranged. Now *that* was how a church should look. William pitied Lawrence and the awful Mass he was sure to endure. They'd talk later. Poor boy.

"For all the thoughts and prayers that are in our hearts, we pray to the Lord," he said.

"Lord, hear our prayer."

At Resurrection, Lawrence stood at the altar, assisting as Tom prepared the Eucharist. The ushers passed small baskets for the collection as the choir sang. But the ministry of button-pushing had hit a snag. The congregation, who followed the projected words that shone upon screens on opposite sides of the church, was singing two different verses. The slides were out of sync.

Lawrence, of course, heard the discordance immediately and looked out toward the sides of the church. On the left, the man clicking the button of one slide projector sat, focused intently on his job. On the right, Therese had taken control of the projector and was attempting to catch up. Over the choir's last notes, Lawrence could just hear her hissing at the woman who had been running the projector, could see the expression on Therese's face from where he stood. She was livid. The other woman stood aside helplessly.

Tom finished his prayer and stepped back from the microphone so that Lawrence could continue. "Let us give thanks to the Lord our God," said Lawrence, with more Christmas cheer than he'd felt all night.

At St. Justin Martyr, Rob said the words of the Eucharistic prayer, held aloft the consecrated Host, genuflected at the altar in quiet dignity. The church was full. Jessica had found a seat in the middle of a pew. By holding her head at just the right angle, she could see Father Rob as he led the community in prayer.

Father Rob's white vestments gave him the look of a medieval saint, a carved marble statue. The thick brocade hung in alabaster folds as he extended his arms toward the congregation, inviting them to pray. Perhaps the flickering candles and the lingering smoke of incense fooled her eyes, but she imagined she could see, as Father Rob lifted the chalice and the consecrated wafer, the bright glow of some holy aura around him. A shiver of awe tingled up her spine. She bowed her head to pray.

At St. Cecile, Father Cesar Castro stood aside as Monsignor Grimmley said the Mass. Monsignor had ignored Cesar's offer to concelebrate or even read one of the Scriptures during Mass. Yet Monsignor had also declined Cesar's request to celebrate Mass elsewhere. Cesar's only apparent task was to stand there and look pretty, he thought.

Monsignor rushed through the liturgy with his typical lack of grace; as he prepared to end the Mass, perhaps in a nod to Christmas spirit, he gestured to Cesar. Cesar, startled, stepped to the microphone.

"Bow your heads and pray for God's blessing," he said, and stepped back.

Monsignor pushed in front of the microphone again and blessed the parishioners abruptly, "FatherSonHolySpirit, Mass-is-ended-go-in-peace."

Cesar closed his eyes in disgust.

Mother of God.

After midnight Mass, Jessica genuflected in the aisle, as she had learned to do, and turned to leave. A hand gently grasped her shoulder from behind. She startled and whirled around. "Oh! You surprised me!"

Father Rob smiled. "Sorry! I just wanted to wish you Merry Christmas."

"Thank you."

They paused for a moment, jostled together in the crowd that pushed down the aisle toward the doors. Jessica felt tongue-tied and awkward. She made an effort, but they both spoke at once. "I—"

"Go ahead."

"I was just asking what you were doing for Christmas. Going home?" She flushed, hot in her wool sweater and the crush of people.

"Yeah, home to Mother." He laughed ruefully.

"Me, too. The family Christmas thing."

"Families can be so nutty. Especially at Christmas."

Jessica half-shrugged. "I guess so."

"Well. No RCIA meetings for a few weeks," Father Rob commented. "We'll see you in January, I guess, or at Mass before then?"

"Sure." Someone called the priest's name from behind them. Jessica hitched her purse up on her shoulder and smiled. "I'll let you go. Have a nice Christmas."

Father Rob leaned over and gave Jessica a chaste kiss on the cheek. "Merry Christmas."

"Bye."

She felt the burn of his shadow like a hot slash on her cheek all the way home.

CHAPTER THIRTEEN

Lawrence drew through the beads of condensation on the side of his glass, then licked his dewy finger. It felt cool on his tongue. Around him, men laughed and jostled, and the dance music pulsed with heavy bass. His eyes grew used to the dimness of the bar; he sat with his drink and watched the gaiety of New Year's Eve develop around him.

Men passed, their arms entwined. Lawrence smelled sweat and breath and heat and leather, the unmistakable scent of men on the prowl. He arched his back in a cat stretch, and eased himself off the stool. He shouldn't have come.

But he'd had to get out of the rectory, away from her. Only one day back from his short vacation, and Therese was driving him up the wall already.

Christmas Eve had been bad enough. But the Christmas Day Family Mass was even worse. Therese directed the children's choir to perform a medley of Hanukkah and Kwanzaa songs, with some kind of yoga chanting thrown in. In fact, the name of Jesus wasn't sung once in the Family Mass music selections. Therese's choice for meditation music after Communion was the Walt Disney favorite, *When You Wish Upon a Star*. Lawrence sat before the parishioners in the presider's chair, his hands folded prayerfully in his lap, and a pleasant expression cemented on his face.

When Mass finished, after greeting parishioners outside in the brisk Christmas Day chill, Lawrence caught up with her in the sacristy. Therese pointed at the altar servers' robes that had slid from their metal hangers onto the floor. "You better pick those up before they get too wrinkled."

Her command caught him by surprise, and he responded sharply. "Thanks for pointing that out. You couldn't pick them up?"

"Why do you assume that *I*, as a woman, am responsible for picking up after the children? And by the way, I didn't see you singing at Mass."

"This is Christmas, Therese, Christmas. This isn't some hippie love-in. We're Catholics; this is what we *do*—we worship Christ on Christmas. We don't have to apologize for that!"

"Who's apologizing? Don't you want inclusivity? Are you opposed to celebrating the multicultural diversity of the parish?" She stood, hands on hips, a malevolent elf, and stared up at Lawrence.

"Therese, that's not the point. On Christmas we celebrate the birth of Christ, not the United Nations. Why couldn't we sing about Jesus?"

She turned away. "I can't argue this with you. Obviously you're stuck in the Dark Ages. Priests!" She stalked out the sacristy door.

Lawrence allowed himself a whispered moment of pure profanity. He felt somewhat better as he picked up the altar servers' robes and hung them neatly in the closet where they belonged. He went back to his room and packed some clothes for his short Christmas vacation home to La Jolla. As Lawrence drove away from Resurrection toward the airport, he deliberately locked Therese out of his mind.

But she was still there, prickly, invasive, enmeshed in his daily life like a burr, when he returned.

At the bar, as Lawrence turned to put on his warm tweed coat, his hand caught in the sleeve and he stood there a moment, his arm ridiculously trapped in an awkward position behind his back. He flapped his arm, tried to untwist the sleeve. Behind him, a hand straightened the sleeve, and Lawrence's arm slipped through. The arm rested gently across his shoulders an instant, then dropped. "Thanks," Lawrence said, turning to face his rescuer.

The blue-eyed man with the square jaw shrugged, smiled the thanks away. "You're not leaving, are you?"

Lawrence noted the straight blonde hair that fell across those riveting eyes, the clean white shirt, the dark slacks. A silk necktie, subtly patterned, was Windsor-knotted, and the top button of the shirt, buttoned. The hands, strong and capable, were planted, one on the bar and the other on his hip. Lawrence considered very briefly—there was nothing wrong with having a drink, after all. He put out his hand. "No, I'm not leaving yet."

The man's hand slipped warm into his own grip. The grasp was firm.

"I'm Lawrence."

"Nice to meet you, Lawrence. I'm Jeffrey."

"My pleasure."

Later, Lawrence blushed at his actions, how he had danced until midnight, shrieked with joy at the New Year, hugged and kissed total strangers around him, and in the morning, awoken in Jeffrey's bed, the crisp cotton sheets gone limp under the tumble. He remembered everything. He knew what he had done. He just couldn't adequately justify how he, a Roman Catholic priest, could let himself abandon all reserve, all decorum, and so glibly disremember his chastity. He never even told Jeffrey he was a priest. Better not to talk about it now, though. He sat up and rubbed his eyes. Lawrence could hear the other man showering in the bathroom. The smell of perking coffee drifted from the kitchen. Lawrence felt his stubbled face, mortified by his tousled hair and morning breath, his wrinkled clothes where they lay in shameful abandon. He arose and pulled on his trousers and shirt, felt like a transient in the creased clothing. He couldn't find one of his socks. Lawrence hated to leave it there, knew that some time, eventually, Jeffrey would find that solitary gray sock and think of him. He stuffed the other one in his coat pocket before Jeffrey came back.

They drank coffee in the kitchen of the studio where Jeffrey lived, looking toward San Francisco Bay and the fog-shrouded hills beyond. Lawrence felt a little hung-over and shy. Jeffrey respected the silence, and when the coffee was gone, Lawrence stood.

"I hate to just rush off like this. But—well, you know. I've got to work." His words sounded shallow.

But Jeffrey smiled his cover-boy smile. "I'm glad we met. Maybe I'll see you again sometime." His voice was noncommittal, casual. Lawrence wasn't sure whether to feel relieved or affronted.

They hugged and said goodbye. They did not exchange numbers or info. Lawrence swung his car onto the wet city streets, made his way to the freeway, and headed south through misty rain toward the Peninsula. He bypassed his exit, though, and continued a few miles farther; Lawrence didn't stop until he had pulled his car into the driveway of the rectory at St. Justin Martyr, next to Rob's rain-spattered Jeep.

He walked up the front path through the muddy, barren garden. He knocked, and greeted a surprised Rob with a sheepish grin. "Happy New Year. Can I come in?"

"Sure." Rob, in jeans and a sweater but still-bare feet, held the door open. "Happy New Year." He glanced at Lawrence's wrinkled clothes and stubbly face, and gestured with his cup. "Want some coffee?"

"Yeah," Lawrence said. He stepped in, rubbing his face. "In a minute. But first, will you hear my confession?"

Ordinary Time

CHAPTER FOURTEEN

Father Philomel Lacaro's church, St. Ambrose, had been built in the late 1960s during a post-Vatican II fever of questionable architecture; the result was an A-frame church that looked like a Swiss chalet. The priests of the diocese dubbed it "The House of Pancakes," which suited Phil's sense of the absurd. After attending the Chrism Mass for the Blessing of the Oils at the Cathedral, the boys gathered at his invitation in the pine-paneled rectory behind St. Ambrose.

Rob and Lawrence joined William and Cesar in Phil's living room, with its two battered recliners and sticky vinyl sofa. At the green-speckled kitchen counter Phil sorted through a vast collection of take-out dinner menus, searching for the ultimate Chinese food. On one long wall hung a large mosaic of the Last Supper, entirely made of dried legumes; Jesus' robes were crafted in gray-white navy beans, St. Peter's beard was of yellow split peas, and Judas Iscariot's perfidious face was the greenish-white hue of dried limas. On other walls hung the annually issued parish calendar, a poster of Popeye's friend Wimpy, and a blown-up photo of Phil being ordained by the Most Reverend Paul Cornelius, bishop of the diocese.

Lawrence knelt by the stereo console to examine Phil's musical selections, clucking as he looked. "Jeez, Phil, you still have your 8-tracks?"

"How about a little drinkie, boys?" William rummaged in the fake-pine-fronted bar cabinet. "Do you mind?" he asked Phil over his shoulder.

"Be my guest." Phil found the menu he wanted and tossed it on the scarred Formica dinette table. "Go for it, boys. Hey, have you guys heard about that nun's book that just came out?"

"What nun's book?"

"Some Feminazi-nun wrote a book on why women should be ordained. It's all about the evil patriarchy."

"Yeah, Therese has been talking about it nonstop at my place," Lawrence said, looking over Phil's albums. "She's ready to take up arms, she said." He fake-gagged. "Spare me."

"The Bishop won't like that," Cesar said.

"No shit, Sherlock," Phil said, laughing.

William finally found an acceptable wine and worked in a corkscrew to open it. He grimaced as he drew the cork; it came free with an exquisite pop. William breathed in the bouquet with an appreciative sniff. "So where's our Patrick these days? Anyone seen him lately?"

From his corner by the stereo, Lawrence looked around at Cesar. "Yeah, where is he?"

"What? What are you looking at me for?" Cesar was wide-eyed. His hand fluttered to his lips.

"C'mon, Gladys. Let's have it."

"Yeah, spill it, Sleazer."

"Well," Cesar huffed. "If you're going to twist my arm, I may as well tell you." He paused dramatically. "He's at Gemma Springs." He smoothed his black clerical shirt, avoiding anyone's eyes.

"Noooo!"

William cackled, "Oh, lovely!"

A surge of guilt swept through Rob. He hadn't heard from Patrick since the last phone call in December, when Patrick had begged him again not to tell about Kate. Rob had reluctantly agreed, but in the manic weeks leading up to Christmas, he hadn't had time to call back to see what Patrick had decided to do. He should have done something more. It was too late now. Always and again, the Catholic prayer arose: *For what I have done, for what I have failed to do—* Rob pictured Patrick out in New Mexico at the treatment center, surrounded by alcoholics, pedophiles and porn-addicted priests. "What happened?"

"Somebody complained." Cesar sat back in a tweedy recliner.

"Not you, of course," Rob said.

Cesar looked up at Rob. "I give you my word."

William brought a tray of wine glasses to the burled walnut stump coffee table. Some glasses were printed with the name of a local wine festival; others looked like prizes from the school festival's coin pitch.

William handed glasses around. "You might as well tell everything, dear," he said, handing Cesar a half-filled glass of Riesling.

Cesar glanced at Rob again, then away. He sipped his wine. "The Sensitive Issues Committee heard a rumor and went to investigate."

"The clergy CIA!" Lawrence whistled. "They meant business."

"Of course." Cesar nodded. "The committee sent someone to watch the rectory and they saw that *woman*—"

"Kate," Rob said. "She has a name."

"Yes, well, they saw her and the baby, and apparently they're still going at it." Cesar brushed at a fleck of lint on his black trousers.

"What? Who's going at it?" Phil plumped his behind on the arm of the couch, entranced.

"She and Patrick. They were *in flagrante*. I saw the report in the Bishop's box. Then I saw *him*. The Bishop called him in, and Patrick admitted it was his son. So the Bishop sent him away."

"Gemma Springs! Oh, Paddy, you naughty boy!" William raised his glass to Patrick. "Does the Bishop really think it'll cure Patrick of his evil ways?"

"I doubt it. The Bishop sent him there to think and to pray. To get over her." Cesar sipped his wine. "Don't ask me. I just work there."

"He won't get over her," Rob said quietly.

"You don't think so? I do." Phil laughed. "There's always some other collar-clipper around the corner."

"Let's order," Lawrence said quickly. "How about something spicy? Who likes garlic chicken?"

The others gathered around the menu and made their choices, while Phil speed-dialed the restaurant. Rob walked across the room to the window and looked out at the rock and juniper landscape in the rectory's front yard. He turned when Lawrence approached.

"Rob, what would you like?"

"Whatever." He shrugged. "It doesn't matter."

Lawrence sighed. "I know what you're thinking. Are you going to be okay?"

Rob shook his head. "You don't just get over it. You don't just get over fathering a child with a woman you love."

"I know. But he should never have gotten involved with her. He knew that. It's one of those hazards of the job."

"I realize that. It's just—" They'd had this conversation so many times before. Rob couldn't articulate his feelings, not in a way that would make any sense. It was one thing to tumble with a stranger, and another thing entirely to make a family, to begin a new life with someone. Both were wrong, far outside the boundary of what a priest could do. But he couldn't bring himself to condemn Patrick. "It just doesn't seem fair."

"Of course it's not fair. But we all made the big choice, remember?" Lawrence fingered the thick gold ring from St. Joseph's Seminary on his slender finger. "That's why we're here. Patrick knew the consequences, and he knew he'd get caught. It's totally out of our hands. Just offer it up, Rob, like we always do." Lawrence gestured at Rob's glass. "Have a drink. There's nothing else to do."

CHAPTER FIFTEEN

Rob and Lawrence first met at St. Joseph's Seminary, right out of high school. Both of them melted quickly into seminary life, and into a friendship of opposites. Rob had never been away from home before; Lawrence had been an exchange student for a year in Italy. Where Lawrence's politics were conservative, Rob's were blue collar-liberal. Lawrence came from a large, wealthy family; Rob was the child of a poor widow. Rob studied liberation theology and the effects of Vatican II, while Lawrence bemoaned the loss of the Latin Mass and revered the tradition and rubrics of the liturgy. Their differences made them argue and swear and bait each other, then give way to laughter.

Lawrence at twenty was thin and graceless, tall and growing still taller; he tripped up the marble stairs, dropped dishes in the refectory, and lost handfuls of coins in the frigid silence of the library. Rob never knew where something hot, wet, or indelible would land when Lawrence was around to spill it. But Lawrence's awkwardness vanished in the music room, when he laid his fingers on the organ or gave the full throat of his golden tenor to the choir.

Rob roomed next door to Lawrence in the dormitory. On warm nights after dark, the young men opened the windows and, against the rules, sat on the ledge. Their legs swung three stories above the ground as they talked. Older seminarians could be persuaded to buy a six-pack or a bottle of wine; they passed bottles back and forth until empty and their thoughts ran down, and then only sleep remained. In the morning, Lawrence would rise early to search for one of his shoes or books that had inevitably fallen, or hide an empty bottle before the Sulpician Fathers found it.

During his first years at St. Joseph's, Rob reveled in the company of men, after enduring eighteen years with his mother and her Portuguese mutterings. He played touch football in the meadow with priests and seminarians, snapped towels in the shower, and found community in the bass rumble of laughter among men. The seminary was a masculine fortress, a theological tree house where no girls were allowed. Testosterone was an almost palpable scent in the corridors. If a woman came upon the seminary grounds, heads turned with a single thought: "What does *she* want?" Innuendo punctuated conversations, and in the dormitories, profanity was the *lingua franca*.

In such a masculine environment, a forthcoming pledge of celibacy seemed possible, even easy. The seminarians gave themselves to God and Church, Father and Mother. Rob wholly believed in the solidarity of the brotherhood, the union of his fellow priests, the common ground on which they knelt.

After their first four years of seminary college, the men began the second four years of graduate study for the priesthood, during which they spent time in local parishes, learned how to say Mass, and undertook the many steps toward full ordination. Every man there was steeped in Catholic life, from early breakfast at the refectory to evening prayer in the chapel.

Then suddenly, he was kneeling over Shannon in bed, rocking into her, his eyes closed in guilty ecstasy. Rob spent that summer making love, a nagging guilt in his mind that he fought, and with her, overcame. Clean-scented hair, skin that burnished in the sun, a dew of sweat on the smooth skin of her brow: These he worshiped. They lay under the sun, always a finger touching, or a knee, a thigh. Upstairs in her apartment Rob brought ice water to the bed, watched as Shannon drank in long gulps, dripping from the glass. Then she nuzzled him, her mouth still ice-cold from her drink.

Lawrence had worried about Rob, heard gossip around the seminary.

"Souza's not coming back."

"Nope, he's gone the way of the woman."

"Breeder."

Lawrence tried to telephone, left a note in Rob's dorm room, and finally showed up at Shannon's apartment. Shannon was just leaving; she kissed Rob on the lips as she passed. "Glad to have met you, Lawrence," she said over her shoulder.

"Well, this is nice," Lawrence said, his eyebrows raised, faintly mocking. He looked around at Shannon's apartment, her novels and magazines on the shelves, clothes spilling out from the bedroom closet. Rob's overnight bag lay in a corner. Rob leaned against the kitchen doorjamb.

"It is, actually," Rob said. "Want a soda or something?"

"No, thanks." Lawrence gave up the pretense. "Look, Rob, what are you doing here? Are you gone for good, or is this just temporary —?"

"Insanity?" Rob flicked a look of annoyance at Lawrence. He crossed to the sofa and sat down with the air of a man at home.

"Well?"

"I'm happy here. I'm in love with her." He folded his arms and looked up at Lawrence, still standing near the entry.

"So that's it—you're in love. What about your education? What about your scholarship? Are you going to let all that go?"

"I don't know."

"What are you going to do, then? Live off Shannon's money? Or get some slag job? That'll be fun, raising a family on minimum wage."

"It's not like that." Rob wanted Lawrence to see how good it was, how everything would be fine in the end. "I'll work part-time until I finish grad school, and then get a real job. We're going to get married at some point."

"So what do I tell everyone back at St. Joe's?"

"You don't have to say anything. It's not your problem, and it's not their business." Rob sighed and asked, "Come on, aren't you happy for me, Lawrence?"

Lawrence stared at Rob, incredulous. "I would be if I thought you were doing the right thing. If I thought that you believed it yourself. But I don't. It's too much to ask, for her to expect you to give up everything you've worked for. It's just too much. Put your cock away and take a look around." Lawrence gestured around at the apartment. "Want to know what's wrong with this picture? Where are *you*? You're not even here."

"Is that all you have to say?"

Lawrence walked out.

Rob walked slowly around the apartment, looking at Shannon's things, running a finger across the spines of books, fingering the silky fabric of her dressing gown in the closet. Above Shannon's bed, a hand-carved antique with a massive mahogany headboard, hung a shelf on which had once stood a statue of the Infant of Prague, the plaster of its face crackled with age, its pink plaster hands outstretched in blessing. Rob had been startled by the incongruity of such a traditional, Old World relic, so like his mother's beloved saints, in the apartment of the modern young woman in whose bed he was sleeping.

The Infant gazed on them like a benevolent god, its lips half-parted to reveal two tiny white teeth; its preternatural blue eyes watched them sleep, witnessed their coupling and seemed to referee their quarrels. The Infant of Prague rocked above them as they rolled in the sheets until the mahogany headboard thumped the wall; the statue jiggled dangerously close to the edge of the shelf, and one day, danced right off onto the floor. Its hand was broken, white crumbles powdered the floor, yet plaster still clung to the wires within. Shannon laughed after her shock, then it became a running joke, a lovers' code between them. "Let's go rock the baby," she would whisper, and they'd slip away to the bedroom.

The Infant fell again during lovemaking, and again. The plaster hands crumbled apart, one digit at a time, then the nose, the chalky face eaten away as flesh from a leper, and in its place were left those skeletal gray wires.

Shannon wanted to throw it in the Dumpster, but Rob refused; blessed objects must be buried or burned. He wrapped the Infant in a white dishtowel like a shroud, and buried it furtively in the apartment's garden after dark, as if it were his own secret child.

When winter came, Rob knelt in the church and knew where he belonged, knew too strongly the call he couldn't deny.

"I'm going back," he'd finally told her, then gathered his few things, blinking hard until he was gone, away from her. He walked downtown and waited for the bus, and when it arrived, got on and rode back to St. Joseph's.

At last Rob stood at the gates and looked in at the seminary lights. There was no one in sight. The air seemed hushed, still, as if time stopped within those walls, as if no one need fear in the arms of Church. Outside were all the doubt and grief in the world; he had only to step through. Rob sat on the curb and cried at last, tried to squeeze his heart empty of Shannon and the life she had promised him.

"Why?" he raged in prayer, his head down on his knees. "Why does it hurt so badly if this is where You want me? How could she come into my life if there wasn't a reason? If this was a test, damn it, did I pass or fail?"

His legs grew stiff in the winter chill, in the winter darkness, and his back ached from his crouch on the curb. His tears subsided. Rob kept his head bent, his face shielded from the lights of passing cars, and prayed without words, let a river of pain flow toward God. Slowly, minutely, a finger of something seemed to penetrate his heart, and he began to cry again; Rob raised his head and looked up, feeling the ridiculous urge to laugh. He held his hand over his mouth to suppress it but he couldn't stop, and he let go like a madman, and laughed, "Oh, God, oh, God, no more, I can't." Tears ran down his face, joyous, molten, a baptism of fire and water, pain like a death and resurrection of his faith, the finger at his heart, tapping, *let Me in*. Rob rose on shaking legs. God was near.

"Okay," Rob said aloud, gasping for breath. "Okay, I'm back." He wiped his eyes on his sleeve and walked through the gates of St. Joseph's Seminary.

CHAPTER SIXTEEN

Rob answered the front door of the rectory to a young woman standing with a baby. She carried a bulging yellow diaper bag and a battered purse over one shoulder; her hair blew in the gusty afternoon wind.

"Hi." She looked nervously up at Rob. "Remember me?"

She was still petite but not as slender as she once had been. She had rounded with the pregnancy; her face looked fuller, her arms plumper. Her hair was still corn-blonde, but lank; dark smudges curved beneath her blue eyes. But the baby—to whom else but Patrick could that baby, with that dark hair and those same wide eyes, possibly belong?

"Kate!" Rob pushed the door back, unable to hide his surprise. "Come in, please."

She stepped into the foyer, her bag and purse slipping clumsily from her shoulder. The baby began to cry the harsh bleat of a newborn. Rob took her bag and purse and led her into the warm sitting room, where soft jazz played on the stereo and a fire burned in the fireplace. Rob's papers and books were spread on the coffee table; he had been working on his homily for Sunday. He bunched them together and pushed them aside as the baby's cries intensified.

Kate dropped onto the couch and shrugged out of her jacket one sleeve at a time, rocking the baby with a look of desperation. Rob sat opposite her, on the edge of an easy chair near the hissing fire, watching, unsure how to help. The baby arched its back and rooted at Kate's bosom, wailing loudly.

"I'm sorry," she said over the cries. "I have to feed him. Do you mind?"

She gave Rob a mortified look, and reached for the buttons on her faded blue sweater.

"Oh, of course not, go ahead." Rob all but leapt from the chair. "I'll just make some tea or something." He went to the kitchen and put the kettle on to boil. The baby's wails stopped, and he heard Kate's soft murmur from the sitting room.

He took his time setting mugs and spoons and some cookies on a tray, waiting for the kettle to boil. Rob wasn't a prude about breast-feeding; all his Portuguese aunts and cousins had nursed their babies. But he hardly knew Kate. He'd met her only once, about a year before, when he had stopped to chat with Patrick at Queen of Heaven. Long looks between the priest and the pretty youth minister had aroused Rob's suspicions, but Patrick had denied any involvement at the time.

The kettle whistled. Rob poured scalding water over tea bags in mugs and carried the tray into the living room, humming softly as he walked to announce his presence. The baby was still nursing, but Kate had draped a flannel receiving blanket over her shoulder, hiding the baby's face and her open sweater from view.

"Thanks," she said, as she took her mug in one hand and carefully blew on the fragrant tea. In the pause, she and Rob looked at each other, and then her eyes filled.

"Father Rob, what am I going to do?" She set down the mug and wiped her eyes on her sleeve.

"Have you talked to Patrick since he left?"

"Yeah, he sneaks away and calls me whenever he can. But I'm here, all alone, with no job, no money. I had to quit my job at Queen of Heaven, you know. Now I can't work because I don't have a babysitter; I couldn't pay one, anyway. I need Patrick here to help me! He's in this, too. But the Bishop sent him away, and I just can't do this—" Kate choked into gasping sobs, holding her hand over her mouth. Tears dripped over her hand.

Rob reached over and offered Kate the box of tissues, then turned away, bending to put more wood on the fire, hiding his anger. How could Patrick leave her like this? And shame on the Bishop for sending him away, neglecting Kate and the baby altogether.

Until Kate, Rob hadn't thought Patrick would get involved with women. At the time, Rob had listened to his friend's confession without comment. Who was he to judge? However foolish Patrick's choices, Rob had felt some sympathy for his friend. But now, with Kate crying in his own living room, Rob cursed himself for his silence.

"Kate, I'm so sorry about this. Let me make some phone calls and see what we can do for you."

She sniffed and nodded.

"I'll be back in a few minutes," he said, and went to his office. Rob dialed the vicar of finance for the diocese. They spoke quietly of the situation. It was more prudent for the diocese to send Kate a monthly child support check, Rob suggested, than for Kate to call a lawyer, or to go public with the story. The vicar agreed.

"Any idea when you'll bring Patrick back from New Mexico?"

"I can't speak to that as of this time," said the vicar curtly, and hung up. Rob had a feeling Patrick would be heading back soon to face whatever other penance the Bishop might give him. Rob went back up the hall.

The baby lay asleep on the couch next to Kate, the flannel blanket covering his hunched-up bottom.

"Okay," Rob said softly as she turned to him. "The vicar says you'll start receiving a monthly check this week, and it should be enough to cover your expenses. But let me know if there are any problems. I'll do what I can to intercede, okay?"

"Thank you so much, Father." She stroked her child's tiny round head as he slept. "He looks like Patrick, doesn't he?"

"He does." Rob leaned against the mantel, the fire hot on the back of his jeans. "Now that that's settled, I think we need to talk." He cleared his throat. "Kate, are you really going to wait around for Patrick to leave the priesthood?"

She looked up, her expression hopeless. "I don't know. I want him to be with me—with us," she corrected herself. "But he said he can't leave. He has no way to support us. He's scared of the publicity and the backlash. He'd be excommunicated, and his mother would just die!"

"You have to do what's right for you and the baby," Rob said. "If Patrick won't leave, then you're on your own, unless you want to be his mistress, and try to raise your son like that?"

She hesitated. Rob waited while she thought, waited for the reality to sink in. Kate finally shook her head, tears pooling in her eyes again.

"Because it is a stigma, Kate, even in this day and age. As long as he's a priest, there's no way the Bishop will allow you to be together like a family.

Of course Patrick will want to see his son. But there's bound to be all sorts of fallout. It won't be pretty."

Kate fondled her son's dimpled hand. Tears slid down her pallid cheeks.

"I'm really sorry, Kate. I don't want to have to say all this to you. But the fact is, Patrick left you in this position, and here we are, trying to pick up the pieces. Look, I can't tell you what to do. You both have your choices to make. And if he doesn't choose you, you'll have to find a way to make it on your own."

"I know," she said, more to herself than to him. "I'm just so scared."

"I'll do what I can to help." He offered her the tissue box again.

She took one and wiped her eyes. "Thanks, Father. You saved my life today."

"No, just pulled some strings. And made you cry." He smiled. "I'm sorry."

"It's not your fault." She gave back a watery smile. "I needed to hear all that. I really did. Thank you."

Kate got up and hugged him, and Rob blessed the child, whose name was Matthew, and whose gray eyes and dark brow looked so like Patrick's. Rob wrote her a check from his own account and made her take it, to tide her over. He stood in his shirt sleeves in the cold wind and waited as Kate got into her car, strapped the baby into his infant seat, and drove away into dusk.

Rob walked around the rectory to the back of the church, unlocked the priests' door and went in. He went through the sacristy, past the cupboards with chalices and sacramental wine and altar cloths, past the closets hung with vestments and banners, out into the dim, empty sanctuary. No one else was there at dusk on a Wednesday, only the red sanctuary lamp's flame that showed the eternal presence of the Holy One. Rob reached back for the panel of light switches, then changed his mind, and walked into the hollow quiet of the empty church, its darkness mitigated by the flicker of votives in the alcoves.

He walked to the front of the church, centered himself before the large crucifix, and genuflected. The gray silence seemed to press on him like a hand, and he brought both knees to the carpeted floor. No words formed in his mind, only images: Kate's tears on her tired face like the Sorrowful Mother, the baby's lips nursing at air as he slept, the glance Rob had witnessed between Patrick and Kate that one time. The wrongness of their situation gripped him, how unfair it was to every party. Kate wanted a family, the Bishop wanted his priest, Patrick wanted both for himself, and the baby Matthew had no choice at all. No one could win, unless someone else lost.

Rob knelt in the hush and dark of church and let his heart pray without words. As always, God was listening.

CHAPTER SEVENTEEN

Rob stood at the back of the church just before ten-thirty Mass, waiting for the music to begin. Parishioners bustled into pews as the choir director announced the opening hymn and invited the congregation to sing. Rob fingered his collar and shrugged under the weight of the heavy linen chasuble, deep green for Ordinary Time, the interval between Christmas and Lent.

An altar boy lifted the cross on its pole and led the procession up the aisle. Two more altar servers followed. A lector hoisted the Lectionary above her head and followed the children up the aisle, walking in step to the hymn.

As Rob joined the procession, a flash of chestnut hair caught his eye, and he knew without turning his head that she was there. When he reached the front of the church, he bowed before the altar, went around and kissed the altar stone, then took his place at his chair, and sang the remaining verses with the congregation. His eyes slipped toward the back of the church.

Jessica had come into church right behind him and found her seat near the back. She always sat there, near the statue of St. Margaret, virgin martyr. Dozens of votive candles flickered around the statue's base, where a dragon twined under Margaret's cold marble foot. From where Rob stood, the candles lit a penumbra around Jessica's hair. He felt a protective pull toward her, almost paternal, as he sometimes felt with parishioners in need. She seemed fragile as glass and yet unbroken, full of story that she couldn't share, a message in a bottle, still drifting. He almost wanted to hold her, cradle her and rock her like a baby, let her shed unspent tears. But he couldn't do that.

Rob began the Mass, his voice amplified and resonating through the church. "In the Name of the Father, and of the Son, and of the Holy Spirit." In her seat by St. Margaret, Jessica crossed herself, her eyes closed.

Although he said the prayers, listened to the readings, sang the proper responses, Rob couldn't keep his mind wholly on the Mass. He glanced through the church, scanning the familiar faces of parishioners, the old ladies in the front pew, the Filipino family on the aisle, the mentally ill man who talked to himself in the chapel. Rob's eyes rested at the back of the church. She looked up from her missal and met his glance. He shifted his focus away, watched a crying baby as its mother carried it out, and brought his mind back to the Mass as the choir began to sing *Alleluia*. Rob said his homily and consecrated the wafer and wine; he stood at the front to distribute Communion, the same motions, a mechanical pace. He held the small papery discs of wheat wafer, the consecrated Jesus, gave them into the hands of his parishioners.

"The Body of Christ." *Amen.*

"The Body of Christ." *Amen.*

He waited with a schoolboy's expectation for her face in the long line of faces, dark, old, pale, weathered, bored, reverent, when of course she wouldn't come up. Jessica had yet to be baptized into the Church at Easter. It was stupid to forget that, ridiculous to feel disappointed. In a brief gap between the shuffling bodies in line, Rob glanced again toward the back. Jessica knelt alone in her pew, her eyes tightly shut and her hands clasped, as if praying for her heart's desire. The line moved and blocked his view. He placed the consecrated wafer into cupped hands.

"The Body of Christ." *Amen.*

And before he had a chance to greet her, she slipped past him again in the crush of bodies eager for the sugar rush of doughnuts after Mass. The little old ladies stopped to shake his hand and ask for his blessing. Children hung on his hands and told him jokes. A member of the liturgy committee intercepted Rob as he turned to look for the nimbus of hair, the downturned face, and Rob stood and listened as the man complained about the outcome of a previous meeting. When at last Rob might have had a moment to speak in relative peace as the cars roared out of the parking lot, she was already long gone.

Rob went inside the church, straightening missals and rescuing a lost sweater from beneath a pew, stray tissues from the floor, then into the sacristy to remove his vestments. He had an hour before the last Mass of the day, and walked back through the garden to the rectory in search of coffee. The gardener had pruned the rose bushes down to thorny canes, but green blades of spring bulbs had begun to thrust through the loamy soil. In the rectory, Rob poured himself a cup of coffee and sat at the pine table to look at the Sunday paper. But he couldn't read, sat instead with his coffee cooling and his eyes unfocused, thinking of fingers splayed to rake her hair, a wild tumble of copper light.

Rob closed his eyes and swept the images away like an erasure, chastised himself for the indulgence. He said a part of the secret prayer of priests, the silent prayer before Communion that he often said to himself, "By Your holy Body and Blood, keep me free from all my sins."

The telephone rang. Rob waited, sipping lukewarm coffee, while the answering machine clicked on at the second ring. His own voice noted the times of weekday and Sunday Masses, and invited callers to leave a message.

"Robert, it is Cesar. Pick up the phone, you lazy man, I know you are there!"

Rob grinned and got up to answer the phone. "Sleazer, you dog! Why aren't you saying Mass?"

"I have ten minutes before Mass. Listen, Robert. I heard some talk about you down at the diocese."

"The Bishop's office? About me?" Rob set down his mug. "Like what?"

"The Judicial Vicar wants to move you from St. Justin. He wants you in the Canon Law office." Cesar clicked his tongue. "You could go to Rome to study, my friend. Think of the opportunities!"

"But I haven't even been here six years! I haven't served out my term as pastor yet." Rob stared at the crumbs that remained on the counter top from his breakfast toast. "Are you sure? I can't leave here now, right in the middle of RCIA and everything." Rob swore under his breath.

"Relax, Robert. Nothing is final. There was some talk, that's all. Someone will call you if they're serious. And you can always turn them down, you know."

"Yeah, sure I can."

"I'll let you know if I hear anything else."

"Thanks for the heads-up, Cesar." Rob hung up the phone and sat down. The he stood up again and walked to the window, looked at his garden, looked around at his rectory kitchen. His butter knife, his empty cup in the sink. He had dwelled in his loneliness for nearly six years at St. Justin Martyr. The rectory had been his home, however empty, and suddenly he didn't want to leave it. He didn't want to go to Rome or work in the stultifying Canon Law office. And though he couldn't admit it to anyone save his guardian angel, he didn't want to go away and leave St. Justin, its clean white walls and marble saints, and candles flickering in a halo of copper hair at the back of the church.

CHAPTER EIGHTEEN

"Moral choices are not always clear-cut," Father Rob told the catechumens. "Sometimes right and wrong are not opposites, like black and white. For example, is it always wrong to kill?"

Around Jessica, the people nodded their heads, no question about it. She sat like a statue, unable to move or turn away.

"The Church teaches that to kill someone is a sin. That's why the Church is opposed to abortion, euthanasia, and the death penalty. We believe that life is precious and must be protected. But what if you have to kill in self-defense? That's something you wouldn't choose to do, but might be forced into; the Church would say it's wrong, but in that case it might not be a sin."

A hand rose. "What if you don't know it's wrong?"

"Children often do things, like tell lies or take things, before they understand the difference between right and wrong. We don't count that as sinful. The knowledge of sin must be present," Father Rob explained. "When you do something deliberately wrong, when you understand that it's wrong and you do it anyway, we call it a sin."

I understand, Jessica thought. *Knowledge of sin*. The phrase seemed so Old Testament, so Adam-and-Eve, with apples of knowledge and coiling serpents. *He had known her, in the Biblical sense.* What she knew of sin could fill a book, or several.

"There are other forms and degrees of sin," the priest continued. "In the prayer called the *Confiteor*, we confess that we have sinned 'in my thoughts and in my words, for what I have done and what I have failed to do.' That's called a sin of omission, like not speaking up when you know there is evil or wrongdoing. We ask forgiveness for what we have *done*, and what we have *failed to do*."

Other hands rose, and Father Rob called names, answered questions. Jessica sat in a folding chair next to Susan, her sponsor, shame rising like nausea, until the meeting ended. Mutely, she followed the group to the hospitality room and took a slice of cake, though she didn't want it. Sins of silence, commission, omission. Penance and purgatory. Abstinence and ashes. She had come to the Catholics because they understood suffering. But what was the limit to their tolerance? What was too heinous to forgive?

The sweet clung like paste in her mouth. Her vision blurred. Jessica dropped her cake into the garbage can and walked out the door. She couldn't go on like this, couldn't pretend she was there honorably, had any right to be there at all. She had to tell him everything.

Next day, she called.

"Father Rob? This is Jessica Elliot." She gripped the phone in her hand and tried to lighten her tone, but it came out too loud, fake-cheerful, and she hated the sound.

"Hi, Jessica! How are you?"

"I'm all right." She knew her co-workers were listening, or might be. She lowered her voice. "I'm sorry to bother you like this. But I need to come and talk to you about something."

"Is everything okay?"

She pictured him worried about her, no, annoyed by the interruption, the noise and mess of someone's hopeless dysfunction. But no, that was his job. And she had to say it. He had to hear her.

"It's just something I need to talk about before I go any further in the RCIA program." She held her fingers to her lips, pressed down fear. She breathed again, moved her hand away. "I mean, you might not want me to come anymore."

"Jessica, there's nothing that you can tell me that would make me want you to stop coming." His voice came through the phone, strong and reassuring. But that was what she wanted to hear; maybe she heard him wrong. She couldn't tell anymore. Never knew what to believe.

"No matter what it is, you're welcome here, always. Please know that," he said. A pause. "Listen, my calendar is clear this evening. When do you get home from work? Can you make it over here about six thirty?"

"Maybe. With the train, sometimes I'm late."

"Let's make it seven o'clock. I'll see you here then, okay?"

That evening, straight off the train from work, Jessica drove to the rectory. She walked up the curving path to the front door, between cropped rose canes that, in the winter gloaming, were black and skeletal. Some early-blooming azaleas flowered ghostly white in the dim cast of streetlight. She reached for the brass knocker on the paneled door; her skin looked sallow in the porch light but the door swung open as she reached, and she pulled her hand back.

Father Rob stood with a cup of coffee in his hand. "I saw you drive up. Come in." He stepped back. His clothes were casual, jeans and a white polo shirt.

She stepped into the rectory foyer, with its tiled floor and white walls. On the wall hung a large silver mirror; below it stood a polished table and umbrella stand. A formal portrait of the Bishop gazed severely from its ornate frame. She felt the prelate's eyes upon her, and her skin rippled with chill.

Father Rob appeared not to notice. "Do you want some coffee? I just made some."

"Yes, please." Jessica followed him up the short hall to the kitchen, so clean and simple, with its long counters, cool vinyl floor, a pine breakfast table; she longed for such a large workspace to make her preserves. Red apples filled a blue and white bowl on the counter. He got a white cup from a cabinet and filled it from the steaming pot.

"Do you want cream or sugar?"

"Cream, please." Father Rob took a carton from the refrigerator and a spoon from a drawer, setting them on the counter for Jessica. She felt the heft of the spoon, the chill of the pint, saw the white spilling into dark, a spun galaxy of stars, obliterating her reflected face. She stirred, lifted the spoon and licked it, the metal hot on her tongue. But she felt so cold. She set the spoon in the empty sink and turned to follow the priest to his office.

She sat in a comfortable chair, he in another near her, not behind the old desk that was neat, uncluttered. A photo of his ordination hung on the wall; Father Rob, in white, was on his knees, the Bishop with his white robes cupped both hands in blessing on the young priest's bowed head. On another wall hung an enlarged photograph of Father Rob lighting a candle;

its golden light suffused the picture, cast the shadow of a cross behind him. The picture had appeared in last year's newspaper at Easter, and was what had drawn Jessica to St. Justin the first time.

Father Rob sipped his coffee and set the cup on his desk. "So. What's on your mind?"

She couldn't talk. Words seemed beyond her. When she was twelve, she dug in the garden, turning gray-brown dirt, with a packet of seeds in her overall bib. She forked over a chunk of earth, and saw the wriggling pink bodies, tiny mouths as gaping black holes, blind hairless babies naked in the harsh sunlight. She had turned up a nest of moles, and she couldn't put them back. The babies seethed and roiled, scrabbling blindly with their flippers like mashed human hands, wormlike faceless faces. She couldn't save a single one. Her scent tainted them, the mother wouldn't touch them now, and she had to leave them there, slowly purpling into death, or bury them alive, or let the cats finish them off. Nothing she could do was right. She had pulled some long dry grass over them, and run from the garden, the sight inhumed in her memory.

"It's hard to say," she finally said, to fill the pause. He waited comfortably. She rubbed her hands on her thighs to warm them.

She tried. "I have to ask you something, something critically important to me. But I have to tell you a little bit of history first, give it some context so it all makes sense, if that's okay."

"Take all the time you need."

She drew a shaky breath. "I grew up out in the country, up in Sonoma. It's beautiful there, so green when it rains, so brown in summer. We had horses and cows and sheep, all that country stuff. But as I grew older, I couldn't stand being such a hick, being stranded away from my friends out in the boondocks. I couldn't wait to get out of there. As soon as I graduated from high school, I took off for the big city, and started college in San Francisco. It wasn't that far from home, just an hour away, but it was another world for me, on my own. I loved it."

Father Rob nodded, watching her.

"While I was there, in my senior year, I was supposed to work on a project with this guy from a class. He was cute, and I kind of liked him. So I invited him over to study. My roommates weren't home, and he misunderstood me or something." She stopped. The office was too silent; she held her secret like an egg over the fire, cracked, ready. She felt her face flush again, her heart beating too fast. "He raped me."

"Oh, no, Jessica." Father Rob closed his eyes. "I am so sorry."

He pitied her; she could see herself through his eyes, pathetic and afraid. Her legs felt cramped from forcing them still, preventing them from shaking. She made herself speak. "There's more."

"Go on." He sat, watching her, his legs crossed, his arms folded across his chest. Protecting himself against the stain of her.

"I never told anyone because I felt like such an idiot, such a fool. How could I have been so gullible? How could that have happened to me? I'm supposed to be so smart—how could I have been so naive? I should never have trusted him." She shook her head. "So I never even told my roommates."

"Jess, surely you see that it wasn't your fault. You must believe that," Father Rob said. "No one would want that, or would have expected that, and in every way, he was terribly wrong. You can't blame yourself. You can't."

But I do. She sat without answering for a moment, clasped her hands together to keep them from shaking, from grabbing her purse and running through the door. "So I went on. I went to great lengths to avoid ever seeing him again. But it wasn't that easy to just get over it." She paused, readied herself. Dove in.

"I found out a few weeks later that I was pregnant. I was carrying the child of that *animal* who had already ruined my life. And I couldn't stand it, I wanted to kill myself, I wanted to scratch my own skin off. I couldn't make the appointment fast enough. I went to a clinic and had an abortion."

The tiny tick of Father Rob's watch seemed to fill the room. He looked at her as if frozen, sitting in judgment that would save or condemn her. But he did not speak.

"Everything about it was wrong, but I hated the thought, I couldn't stand it." She squeezed her eyes shut, remembering. "As I sat there in that horrible office, the clinic nurse got out her little circle, this little wheel that she turned to see how pregnant I was, and she says to me, 'Your baby will be born on March 3.' March 3. So now for the rest of my life, I have to remember that my baby's birthday is March 3. Then she gave me a Valium and I went into the next room and that was that."

A man's hearty voice. *Just lie back now.* Sucking, slurping noises, like the last bit of juice through a straw. Red ran up the tube, twisting from her cramped gut out into a jar that the nurse neglected to take when she left the room; when Jessica stood to dress, the same red ran down her legs, and the jar sat on the counter like the accusation that it was, *you, you, stupid bitch, murderer, mommy.*

She looked at Father Rob, the trace of shadow on his face, his expression impossible to read.

"So I'm here to ask you if you'll still let me to come to RCIA. If I can still come here. I mean, does the Church want somebody like me?"

It seemed like forever, an eternity in an instant, but he answered, "More than ever, Jessica."

They sat in silence; he watched her, she felt his eyes on her, but it didn't hurt, it didn't frighten her, he wouldn't hurt her. Yet there was still more to say.

"But how can I go on, how can I get past this? I don't know how to confess, how to cleanse this from me. I've prayed, over and over, I've asked for forgiveness, I've begged, if He would even just *look* in my direction, just give me a sign that He was listening. I don't know how to know if I'm forgiven. How many times do you have to ask, to know that your sins are forgiven?"

His eyes looked toward the wall, and when she turned to follow his gaze, she saw the parish calendar, the color photograph of the church at the top. He spoke hesitantly, thinking aloud. "You know you're going to be baptized at Easter. We believe that baptism washes you clean of all sin. And we're going to have a penance service before then in RCIA."

She nodded.

"But maybe it's best if we just do this now. I want to tell you a story, just a little one, and I hope you don't think it's trite. But I think it might help."

She folded her damp hands in her lap.

"A man was walking along the road, and met another man who said he was Jesus. He asked, 'How do I know you're Jesus?' And Jesus said, 'Ask me anything, and I'll tell you the answer.' So the man says, 'What did I tell the priest yesterday in confession?' And Jesus said, 'I don't remember.'"

Father Rob stopped and looked pointedly at Jessica.

"It was over. It was forgotten. As in, forgive and forget. God is so far beyond our understanding, we can't even imagine. Probably the very first time you even felt your remorse, you were forgiven."

"I've been carrying this with me for so long." Her voice felt thick in her throat. "For five years."

"Lay it down. Let it go."

She drew a choking breath. Breathed it out, let go. She raised her gaze to his. "So I can stay? It's okay?"

He laughed gently. "You're just the kind of person we want here. I think you're exactly the kind of person Jesus had in mind. You're very welcome. Please come to class Tuesday night. I want to see you there."

"Thank you." The forgiveness in his voice was too much. "I'll be there."

"And that was your unofficial first confession." He smiled at her.

Jessica grew pensive again. "What about penance? Isn't there some kind of punishment now?"

"Don't you think you've punished yourself enough?"

She shrugged without answering.

"Keep praying. Keep talking to God. And know that He's listening. Jess, I know this was difficult for you. I'm so proud of you. If you want to talk some more, just call me." He wrote a number out on the back of a blue business card from St. Justin Martyr Catholic Church. "This is my private number. If you call the office here, usually you'll get the answering machine. But if you need to talk, in the evenings or whenever, just give me a call. I really mean it."

"Thanks. I might do that. If you really mean it."

"I do."

"Thank you."

He walked her to the door, and hugged her before she left. The heavy door of the rectory closed behind her. Three, two, one, she made it down the steps before she broke, and tears burned on her cheeks. She walked through dark and tears to her car, got in, put her head against the steering wheel, and let it go.

CHAPTER NINETEEN

Lawrence's hearing was attuned to the nuance of her voice, but the means to block it eluded him. His fingers curled above the keys, unable to play. His shoulders hunched in a perpetual wince. Therese was coming. She was there.

Paper shuffled under the music room's door. More notes. More errata. Minutes from endless committee meetings. Tick-marks next to jobs completed. Question marks next to her unfinished pet projects. The sound of her feet faded up the long hall. He clenched until her presence died away.

At St. Bartholomew, his elementary school, the nuns glided down the waxed linoleum as if they were footless, disembodied angels in black linen. Lawrence played the piano at assemblies, marched his fingers up the keys like soldiers, following the bass and treble notes, the *andante*, the *moderato*, the anthems and marches of the children's hymnal. Sister Marguerite stood behind him, her staff beating time on the floor.

In Sister's hand, the wooden pointer whistled through the air to land upon the skinny backs of boys who dared to goof instead of sing. Lawrence's brother Michael was a frequent offender, but never Lawrence. He was punished on the playground instead.

"Fairy."

"Faggot."

"Queer-bait."

When Father Moriarty came into the room, the children rose. When he left, they sat again, bent to the lesson in multiplication, gave reports on the lives of the saints. "Good job, Lawrence," Father said after every assembly. "Your music is a gift from the angels, you know."

"Yes, Father. Thank you, Father." The hand squeezed his shoulder.

Father Moriarty kept roses. On Saturdays one could see him behind the rectory, in his leather garden gloves and broad-brimmed hat, deadheading the rose hips, forking Grow-All into the black soil. The cement statue of the Blessed Virgin Mary kept watch from her corner of the garden, while birds swooped to the millet scattered at St. Francis's stone feet. A garden hose coiled, green as a snake, on the ground.

"You ever consider becoming a priest, Lawrence?" The parrot-beak of the shears bit the dead wood from the rose tree.

"Yes, Father." Lawrence was twelve, old enough to help around the rectory on a Saturday.

"It's a little early yet, I know. But think about it. It's a good life." Father Moriarty squinted in the sunlight. "A boy like you would do well."

A boy like Lawrence wanted to play the piano instead of Catholic Youth basketball. He stroked the black and white keys, improvised new melodies from the staid lessons he had long surpassed. He read about the lives of the saints, and when he thought of St. Joseph of Cupertino, who could levitate, his fingers ran up the keyboard, and the notes were *vivace*, light and airy. Saints Martha and Mary were dueling melodies, one running downward and the other up; Martha's tune wore itself out cleaning the house for Jesus, while Mary's melody rose as she heard the words of the Savior. When Lawrence contemplated St. Jude, the apostle, patron of lost causes, he began in minor chords, desperate moody tones that wept, yet flickered with hope, grew and expanded until all chords were major, triumphant, crescendoing into answered prayers, and ending *pianissimo*, on the softest note, a grace-filled *Amen*.

Lawrence played his St. Jude absently, mood music for a Therese day. She filled the house. She swept through the parish, superior, intolerant, swallowing his energy. He felt like Jonah, trapped within her. The strange thing was that for all his frustrations, he knew Therese wasn't really the problem. She was surface, a nagging irritation that frenzied him. She was merely a symptom of his inability to focus.

The more he needed to work on his Mass music, the more distracted he was. He supervised the seminarian, Sean, celebrated his own share of the weekday and Sunday Masses, and dealt with the usual frequency of premarital counseling and family crises. Lent had almost arrived with all the madness that accompanied it: special liturgies, the elaborate preparations for Easter. Tom was unsupportive as a pastor, unwilling to pick up the slack, give Lawrence the additional space and time he needed to complete his score.

Therese hung around like a nosy little sister, or worse, a stalking ex-lover; she got in his way, made trouble, teased and tormented him. Rob seemed distant for some reason, like he wasn't really listening when Lawrence called, his mind elsewhere, when Lawrence really needed him, and depended on his friend's sympathy. And beyond it all, the recording contract wavered like a mirage, its grace period melting away.

The problem is the parish. I can't stand it anymore. I've got to get out of here. Lawrence reached for the telephone and dialed the Bishop's office.

CHAPTER TWENTY

As he spoke to the group, her face drew his glance like an apparition, a random splash of oil that shapes the face of the Madonna, and though he turned his eyes away, he couldn't help but see her.

Tuesday nights, Father Rob and the RCIA group met in the gathering room at St. Justin Martyr, their questions more intense and probing as Lent drew near. Rob spoke to them about the Sacraments of Baptism, Confirmation, and Eucharist, and how each represented a milestone in life and made it holy. Though his index cards were aligned on the podium in precise order, Rob rarely referred to them. Instead he scanned the group, caught someone's eye or exchanged a smile as he spoke.

Jessica had never missed a Tuesday class. Rob knew these meetings were important to her, that they helped her find community and comfort. He wanted to encourage her along her faith journey. Since their talk, she had spoken to him frequently, with the intimacy that cathartic confessions sometimes brought. Rob understood the feelings, and didn't fool himself that there was nothing else going on. He had experienced transference before, and knew that sooner or later she would move on. But he couldn't be certain how he would feel when indeed she did.

From behind the blinds in the rectory sitting room, Rob had watched her crying in her car. He had never felt so priestly, yet so impotent, in his life. Since that night, he had been unable to forget her. It was as if he had seen her naked. He found himself wanting to avenge her honor. Rob had always considered himself a rational man, able to forgive the most heinous of sins, but the images in his mind triggered a gut response so animal and ugly that it frightened him. More than ever, he wished her peace, and he prayed for her healing in body and soul.

Then he prayed for his own.

After the meeting, he called for volunteers to help with hospitality and cleanup, but people were busy, tired, hurrying out the doors to get home. Only Jessica stayed to help wash the large silver coffee urn, the cookie trays, and the stainless steel spoons. Rob swept the crumbs from the floor and wiped the tables while she washed. He glanced at her back from time to time, her hair spilling from a loose knot, elbows and shoulder blades angling into the work. Her hands swished the sponge around the belly of the urn as if it were a baby in its bath. When she finished, her hands were pink and soapy. Her nose itched and she rubbed with her wrist, sniffled and scrunched her nose like a child, rubbed it again. Rob laughed at her as he pulled paper towels from a cabinet and handed her one.

The moment exploded, those few seconds stretching immeasurably. He saw her pink, damp hand outstretched, the milky underflesh of her arm as she reached for the towel. He wanted to press his mouth into the crook of her arm, lips against the blue veins, trace them down to the sinews of her wrist. Her fingertips were moist with drops of water that spread into the white weave of the towel, five dots, a crumple as she balled it in her fist. He wanted to curve hard into her hand. Laughter still echoed in the room as he turned to the cupboard, his eyes clouded, to put the broom inside. When he looked again, she had turned back to the sink for a final sponge wipe.

The hospitality room was cleaner than it had to be. Jessica slipped her arms into her coat, dug for keys in her purse. She hesitated at the door. "I can't help asking you," she said. "You seemed distracted tonight. Is something wrong?"

An image of Kate at his door, baby in her arms, crossed his mind. Lawrence's distraught calls about Sister Therese. The phone calls from the chancery office, pressing him to take the new position. "I am a little preoccupied," he admitted.

"Anything serious?"

"I wouldn't call it serious. I guess you could call it an opportunity. I've been offered an assignment in the Marriage Tribunal at the diocese, and they really want me to take it." He watched her face change as he spoke, her soft features set hard, her green eyes open in surprise.

"What? You can't go! We need you here! We're so close to Easter—I don't want some other priest. You have to finish the program with us."

She paused, collecting herself. "Where's the Tribunal—is it a different church?"

"No, the Tribunal's an office at the diocese that handles marriages and annulments, and other canon law issues. Like if a Catholic wants to marry a Protestant, the Tribunal can grant a dispensation for that. The job is totally different from working in a parish. It's like being a lawyer."

"Did you go to school for that?"

"No," he said. "But they think I'm cut out for the job. I'm well organized. And I'm young, relatively speaking." He grinned wryly. "I'd have to go to Rome, or maybe to Catholic U. in Washington D.C. It'd take me a couple of years, and then I'd be a canon lawyer." He thought of classes at the Gregorian in Rome, wet streets of an ancient city, and later, a busy office with piles of cases that needed attention.

The movement of her hand brought him back. She stroked the hair behind her ear, a stray wisp that had escaped from the knot.

"But I declined," Rob said. "I want to be in a parish with people. I asked for an extension on my assignment, so I can be here another six years." The breath that released the tautness of her shoulders was too plain for him. He couldn't encourage her. "You'd better go," he said. "It's getting late."

She looked at her watch, centered on the inside of her wrist, with a twist of her arm, then pulled her purse strap onto her shoulder again.

"Thanks for telling me," she said. "See you." The glass door to the parking lot closed behind her, her shoes brushed the pavement, and soon he saw the headlights of her car swing away.

Celibacy was more than chastity, so much more than sex, he thought. It was everything physical and emotional, every intimate moment that might pass between him and another. Even friendship, *a particular friendship*, as the nuns and priests used to call it, could cross the line. More and more, every little thing he wanted was on the other side. The logic of his feelings defied him. But he pushed them aside like a bead curtain, swept past and left them rattling behind him.

He was a priest. It was simply impossible to get involved.

CHAPTER TWENTY-ONE

In her dream, the water was hot, so deliciously hot. It ran in sheets down her arms, cascaded down her back, played down her breasts, forming tiny waterfalls off her nipples. Jessica stroked her hands through her hair, massaging out the foaming bubbles. Her wet hair was sleek as a seal, mahogany dark in the heated jet of flowing water. Mist rose in the tiled cave of the shower stall.

She reached for the soap, rubbed the bar like a smooth stone against her body, working up a lather against her thighs, belly, breasts. She reached behind her to wash her back, but felt someone there, solid, muscular, male. His hands gently took the soap from her and rubbed her back in circles, slippery hands warm and strong, fingers fine and firm against the ridge of her spine. His hands slipped around her waist, caressed upward, circled her breasts. She closed her eyes and leaned against him, never afraid, safe and clean as a baby, cradled in his arms, warm against his furred chest.

They leaned into the spray, let the torrid flood pour over them, douse away soap. He encircled her with his arms. She turned in his embrace, reached for him, pulled his face down to her.

Jessica opened her eyes, the vestiges of her dream fading. Her room was still dark. She rolled over and checked the clock. 4 a.m. She lay back, relaxed and drowsy, began to drift again.

Her eyes flew open again. In the shower. The man. Father Rob.

Lent

CHAPTER TWENTY-TWO

"This is it," Father Rob told his catechumens in the courtyard of Holy Trinity Cathedral. "This is the last big step before Easter."

On the first Saturday of Lent, the day of the Rite of Election, a special liturgy took place for all of the hundreds of catechumens in the diocese. They gathered together to have their journey of faith witnessed and blessed by the Bishop himself. Every church in the diocese had sent its catechumens, who now assembled in the courtyard, each group bearing its own colorful banner. The cathedral choir began to sing within, and the groups funneled through the open doors, up the long center aisle to their assigned pews.

As Jessica passed slowly up the aisle with the rest of her group, she tilted her head back to see the ornate moldings, the cornices, the turned spindles at every peak, dark and light varnished woods inlaid in the alcoves and arches of the cathedral. Every surface was decorated; her eyes followed curves and angles up to the dim ceiling and down again to paneled walls, and counted the fourteen scenes of the Stations of the Cross. A large crucifix hung suspended above the altar, dwarfing the priests and acolytes below it. The St. Justin group came to its pew and sidled in.

Jessica followed the words of the hymn in the program. She sang with hundreds of voices in the cathedral, while Bishop Paul Cornelius proceeded up the aisle to the front. He was man of average height who looked taller with his white mitre on his head. In his left hand he held a staff and his right hand was upraised, seemingly fixed in a perpetual state of blessing. He was the closest thing to her idea of God that Jessica had ever seen, and there he was, real, walking past her pew, his gray hair wisping out from under the mitre, a mole on his cheek, sweeping past with a royal air, a judge's bearing, and yet a kindness rested in his gray-blue eyes. This was the man who wanted to move Father Rob away from her parish.

Jessica looked toward the front, where Father Rob stood with other priests behind the Bishop, watched him bow his head in prayer. She couldn't imagine St. Justin Martyr without him. Confession with a stranger now seemed unthinkable, and she didn't want another priest to give her Communion. She hated to think of him gone, where she couldn't hear the timbre of his voice in the gathering room, or his blessing at Mass, his words that seemed to reach wherever she needed to be touched. He knew her darkest secret wounds. No one else could share that with her.

The Bishop prayed. The choir sang. Then a priest walked to the podium and began to call the names of the catechumens. One by one, around the large cathedral, catechumens stood. Behind her, and in front of her now, people rose as their names were called. Jessica waited for her name, heard it, and stood. She felt eyes on her back, shivered with goose bumps. Father Rob saw her and smiled, and, heartened, she smiled back. The names rang out until all the catechumens stood, row after row, back through the cathedral.

Father Rob stepped to the podium and addressed the Bishop. "Most Reverend Father, Easter is drawing near. These catechumens, whom I now present to you, are completing their period of preparation. They have found strength in God's grace, and support in our community. Now they ask that after they complete their instruction, they be allowed to participate in the sacraments of Baptism, Confirmation, and the Eucharist."

The Bishop nodded to Father Rob, who stepped back to his place among priests behind the Bishop's chair. The Bishop descended the steps to the front of the church.

Jessica consulted her program. "The Elect will approach the Bishop," it read. One row at a time, the Elect, as the catechumens were now apparently called, slowly filed into the center aisle and up toward the front, where each would be presented to the Bishop.

Jessica didn't know what to say to him. A few feet ahead of her, a woman shook his hand and chatted quietly with the Bishop. Jessica couldn't hear the words. What should she say? The man before her introduced himself and shook his hand.

"God bless you, Bishop," he said, as if the Bishop were in need of that.

"Thank you. Good luck to you. And welcome." The Bishop's voice was a soft growl up close. The man moved away and Jessica was next. The godlike eyes of the prelate rested on her. "Hello," he said. "Welcome."

She responded from the heart. "Are you the one who wants to take Father Rob Souza away from us?"

Bishop Cornelius smiled at her and nodded. "Yes, I am."

"We like him at St. Justin. We don't want to lose him."

"We don't, either," he answered, his smile unwavering.

"Well, if you get tired of him, send him back. He's the best priest there is." Her words hung in the air like a banner.

"Thank you. We know." The smile seemed chiseled on his face. "Welcome." His eyes slipped past to the woman behind her and Jessica stepped away, walked slowly back to her seat. She didn't regret her words. Why would they want Father Rob to leave St. Justin Martyr when he was so integral to the parish? He meant so much to the RCIA group. To her. She couldn't bear the thought of him gone.

After every catechumen had spoken briefly to the Bishop, they sat again, sang again, prayed again. At last he dismissed them, saying: "My dear friends, you have set out with us on the road that leads to the glory of Easter. Christ will be your way, your truth, and your light. Until we meet again, walk always in his peace."

Amen rumbled through the cathedral. Jessica stepped out of the pew and worked her way through the crowd, down the aisle toward the gray light outside the massive arched doors.

Just outside the door, a hand gripped her elbow. "What happened up there? What did you say to him?" Father Rob was at her side, his expression a mix of puzzlement and laughter.

"What do you mean?" Jessica pressed her hand to her throat, as if to take back the words.

"One of the priests overheard you ask the Bishop why he was moving me! He just told me. You've got nerve! It must be the Irish in you." Rob's brown eyes laughed at her.

I'm not Irish, she started to say, but her voice would not obey her that afternoon. "You can't go." The people who pressed around them blurred into white noise, though they laughed and chattered loudly. Everywhere around her were faces, noises, the crush of a crowd, but she suddenly felt as if she were all alone with him, and that every word had immense significance. "You don't know what this means to me."

"Yes, I do." Rob took her hands, both of her hands in his broad palms.

There was so much she wanted to tell him, but she had somehow reached an invisible line, a glass wall, the rail between what could and couldn't be said between them. She knew what was true; she had seen, she hadn't imagined it. He said he knew how she felt, but in that instant, Jessica saw his eyes, raw and honest, and she knew, *she knew* what he felt, too.

"I wish —" But she couldn't say more.

"I know," he said. "Me, too."

CHAPTER TWENTY-THREE

She was there when Father Rob walked into the chapel at St. Justin Martyr at five minutes to seven on a Wednesday morning, still blinking sleep from his eyes.

Jessica saw him halt in surprise and felt his gaze on her for a moment, but she didn't look up. He went into the sacristy, out of sight. She bent her mind to her prayer and tried to blot out the sounds of other worshipers: rustling missal pages, soft steps on the carpet, keys that jangled into a pocket.

This is the day.

She knelt in one of the small pews, her hands folded, her eyes closed, her lips moving slightly. She was dressed in a plaid skirt and a sweater, warm tights and loafers, the grown-up version of a Catholic school uniform that she found herself wearing a lot these days. Her copper hair curled, loose, on her shoulders, a flame beside the dozen gray and white heads of the weekday morning Mass regulars.

Jessica could sense their probing looks. She felt that she had intruded on some private ritual or club of which she was not a member. But the daily Mass was open to all, she told herself. She fixed her eyes on her folded hands, and whispered her intention.

Please watch over...

Father Rob returned from the sacristy, genuflected at the back of the chapel and nodded to his regulars. He wore a chasuble of deep violet for Lent, with a gold embroidered cross. His jeans and white athletic shoes stuck out from under, incongruous. At seven o'clock, he walked up the short center aisle and around the small altar. He began, blessing himself and those in the chapel, "In the name of the Father, and of the Son, and of the Holy Spirit."

Amen.

The weekday Mass was short, maybe 20 minutes or so, unlike the hour-long Sunday Masses she was used to. Jessica was surprised at its brisk pace.

After the *Our Father*, Father Rob said, as always, "Let us offer one another the peace of Christ."

Parishioners turned to greet one another, saying, "Peace be with you." At Sunday Mass, Jessica would shake just the hands of those nearest her. But there were so few people in the chapel at this Mass that everyone greeted one another. Father Rob even came around the altar to shake their hands. Jessica turned to greet him.

"Peace be with you, Jessica," he said, grasping her hand with both of his. He raised his eyebrows, as if to ask, "What brings you here?"

She gave a half-shrug, her hand enveloped in his. "Peace," she said.

When Father Rob distributed Communion, she stayed in her seat, still unable to partake until after Easter. She knelt again, alone, whispering prayers, as the others shuffled up for Communion.

Let it be forgiven.

Father Rob blessed them and the short Mass was over. His regulars chatted with one another, gossiping quietly as they left the chapel. Jessica gathered her purse and coat and went to light a candle before the plaster statue of Mary. Father Rob withdrew to the sacristy to hang up his chasuble.

She slid her donation into the coin box with a clank, lit one of the waxy votives with a long match, and snuffed the match with a thrust into the sand pail. She knelt again, her knees tender from prayer, and committed to memory the scent of sulfur as a mnemonic: *Let me not forget, Blessed Mother.*

There were words she still couldn't say, even to God. Mary was more approachable. She heard Father Rob come out of the sacristy and knew he stood, quietly, at the chapel door. She didn't know what else to pray.

Jessica blessed herself and rose from the kneeler. He was still standing back there. He would want to know. She walked toward him slowly.

"What are you doing here on a Wednesday at the crack of dawn?"

"I took the day off today." She brushed her hair back over her ear.

Although no one else remained in the chapel, she couldn't say it loudly. "Remember my confession?"

Father Rob nodded.

"Today would have been the birthday. March third." She met his gaze, still waiting for the refusal, to be turned out into the street.

But all he said was, "Oh, Jess," and pulled her into a warm, brief hug.

A confluence of images bloomed in her mind. The unbearable pressure of a man's arms around her. The relief of acceptance—or not rejection, anyway. The unexpected tingle of joy. No one was around to see.

She pulled away, embarrassed, and fumbled with her purse strap, her sweater's twisting cable knit, a rusty strand of mane caught in her earring. Father Rob stood there, looking at her with something like compassion, a warmer glow than she deserved. She should go, but the day loomed empty ahead of her.

"You have the day off, you said?"

"Yes."

"Want to go get some breakfast? I don't have any meetings till noon." His smile was kindly. "What do you say?"

Such an offer left her vulnerable. She felt raw and exposed. But there was no agenda in his eyes. No dark plan. Just a friendly offer. She didn't want to ask why, not opening doors with ugly remnants of other bad scenes, going on into light and warmth in a man's eyes, an offer she could refuse, but didn't want to; she wanted to be wanted.

Jessica brushed her hair from her eyes. It was safe with him. It would be okay.

Father Rob drove his Jeep and she followed in her small Honda, parking next to him in the café's minuscule lot.

They were seated across from one another at a table near the window; cars passed with a soft shush that they saw more than heard through the thick glass. They ordered breakfast, and then sat in silence as the waitress poured coffee.

What would they talk about? The hot coffee felt smooth and creamy on her tongue. She swallowed, wondering what to say.

He had told her before that she didn't have to call him *Father*, though most people did. The cradle Catholics, those born into the faith, always said, "Father" when they talked to or about a priest. Jessica didn't have the lifelong habit, and it felt awkward to say, "Father" to someone who was just a few years older than she was. She avoided calling him by name if at all possible.

"Have you eaten here before?" she heard herself ask.

"Yeah, I come here with Lawrence all the time. He's a priest, too. He's at Resurrection, across town. We come here just to talk and eat, and escape the bounds of the collar." Rob stuck his finger into his shirt collar and pretended to choke. "Lawrence is in my support group. He's my best friend."

"What kind of support group?" She almost hesitated to ask; it seemed too personal.

"It's my priest group. There are five of us in it. We were ordained at about the same time. We talk about how to deal with parishioners, or pastors, or different kinds of ministries. Get feedback. Exchange gossip." He sipped his coffee.

"What's it like, being a priest?" Jessica wondered. "I mean, do you have to pray all day? Do you have to give up everything? And if you vowed to live in poverty, how can you afford a car and going out to restaurants and all that?"

Rob leaned back and chuckled deep in his chest. "Ah, it's such a mystery, isn't it? Everyone wants to know the inside story." He laughed again.

"Well, I'll tell you what it's like. I work six days a week, sometimes seven if there's a funeral on my day off. Running a church is kind of like running a small business."

He ticked on his fingers. "I have a secretary who answers the phones and deals with the paperwork. There's a bookkeeper and a gardener. I have a housekeeper who cleans the rectory. There's a music director and a youth minister." He wiggled six fingers at her.

"That's my paid staff. I'm not counting the volunteers; I don't have that many fingers." He folded his hands on the table. "I'm on every committee around here. I marry and bury, I visit the sick, I run the RCIA program, I go to diocesan meetings, and I do a lot of counseling. I'm a therapist, fundraiser, cheerleader, manager, and politician all in one."

"I had no idea," Jessica said.

"Everyone thinks that all priests make vows of poverty, chastity and obedience," he went on. "But that's something out of *The Thorn Birds*. That's Hollywood. I'm a secular—that means I'm a diocesan priest, not a member of an order like the Jesuits. So I didn't pledge poverty at my ordination." His eyes wandered toward the window, watching cars speed past, and then others slow for a red light.

"The diocese provides my housing at the rectory, plus food and insurance. I get paid a monthly allowance, so I can afford a car, my own clothes, and a vacation once in a while."

He stopped when the waitress brought their breakfast: steaming omelets, with sliced melon and strawberries and a basket of warm scones. Rob leaned over his plate and breathed in the scent of hot food. "Mmm, this looks good."

Jessica bit into a strawberry, tasting the sweet red juices. She prompted him, "So you didn't vow poverty. What about your other vows?"

"And I pledged obedience. That means I have to do what the Bishop tells me."

"And chastity?" The word hung in the air, resonant as a gong. She looked down, embarrassed.

"Oh, no."

"What?" She looked up again.

"We don't make a 'vow of chastity.'" He made air quotes with his fingers. "Like I said, that's Hollywood. Oh, and by the way, *everyone* is called to chastity, you and me and teenagers and married people. We're all supposed to be chaste." He sliced the fragrant melon. "What I made was a promise of celibacy."

"What's the difference?"

"Ultimately, the difference between a vow and a promise is academic. It's wording, that's all. I can't get married and have children. No intimate relations, period. That sums up celibacy pretty well." He pulled a smile that might have been a grimace, his gaze on his plate, fingers gripped around knife and fork.

"Are you happy?" It seemed a natural question. "I mean, is it everything you expected?"

Rob waited a minute before answering slowly. "Well, yes, I'm generally content, but no, it's not what I expected." He sipped his coffee, and then went on. "As a seminarian, I envisioned myself as a kind of knight in shining armor, riding in to save unhappy people from the sinful world. I wanted to be a bearer of glad tidings like the Archangel Gabriel. Pretty silly, huh?" He grinned at her.

"I don't think so." She remembered the white aura she thought she had seen around him Christmas Eve, some trick of the light or her tired eyes. He could have been an angel.

"But to be honest, it's hard to feel very holy when I'm trying to get a plumber to unclog the toilet in the men's room, and counsel an engaged couple who should never get married, and write a homily for Sunday. And then it's hard to make the homily sound sincere when I've already said it three times that day." Rob looked at his plate, pushed at bits of egg with his fork.

"But I like what I do. I know God called me to be a priest, and somehow, I still manage to see God in the people. I try to find the holy in the ordinary because that's what God is—a miracle, every day."

"I think so, too," Jessica said. "It feels like a miracle to be here, not here in this café, but here at this place in my life, just getting on with it. I'm so glad I found the Church."

Jessica pushed her plate away, too full to take another bite. She watched him, her chin in her hand. He ate neatly, with good manners, his mouth closed, and his hand in his lap.

"Now tell me about you," Rob said.

"That sounds like a line out of a movie." She smiled, but crossed her arms over her chest. She didn't want to talk.

"No, really. You've been asking all the questions. Are you writing a book or something? Are you a private investigator?"

She gave in. "All right." She tried to think of something interesting about herself. "I grew up in the vineyards up north, like I told you. My parents live up there, still making wine. I'm one of three kids. I have two nieces. A cat. My favorite color is green. I like Mexican food. I'm single. There's not much to tell."

"What else?"

Jessica made a face. What to say? She wanted to be something other than what she was—a glorified secretary, a spinster. "I read a lot for work. I sew." She sounded so boring, she knew, but there was nothing but the truth to tell. "I like music and museums. I do needlepoint. It's not terribly exciting."

"Your life sounds very peaceful," he said. "Quiet. I envy that."

"It's okay, for what it is," she acknowledged. "Someday I'd like to have a nice little house in the country, with a couple of kids, and a dog and a pony, and a big garden full of flowers and vegetables. White picket fence. Apple tree in the yard. That kind of quiet sounds good to me."

"It does to me, too."

The waitress cleared their plates and brought more coffee.

Jessica poured cream and grew a little uneasy, considering. "I want to ask you something."

"Something else?"

"I'm serious."

She straightened in her chair. "What do you think when you see me? Do you think about what I said in your office? I mean, do you look at me and see a—" *Rape victim? Baby killer?* She couldn't finish the thought.

Rob carefully set down his cup. "I see someone who's endured a lot. Someone who's survived some real tragedies in her life," he said. "I don't judge you. I feel a sense of grace within you, if I even think about it at all. Don't worry, Jess."

He slid his hand across the table top toward her like a snake, no, just a hand, his hand, palm down, asking nothing. She sat, stiff, unable to take the hand, to let go of her cup, get a grip, her gaze on the tabletop. It was a brown hand, with a small white scar on one knuckle, a few dark hairs feathering the back. He pulled his hand away and laced his fingers around the white coffee mug again. She had offended him, rebuffed the offer of friendship, of human contact. He would fade from her life before his image could imprint her memory.

Afraid that she had hurt him, she sneaked a glance at Rob. His hands wrapped his cup in a warm embrace. He didn't smile, but his face—brown eyes with the bruised look of olive skin beneath them, a thin shadow on his jaw, his strong brow—the face that he showed her seemed to radiate a message: *Safety.*

Like a fern unfurling in a damp and shady wood, she uncurled her fingers from her cup and inched her hands out, flat, until they spread like pressed flowers on the cool table. She examined them like specimens she was seeing for the first time.

"I have a suggestion for you," he said.

"What's that?"

"Why don't you try to get involved in some of the activities and ministries around the parish? We can always use volunteers, and if you've got some time in your quiet life, why not?"

Why not? She spent too much time alone. A little volunteer work might help her make amends. The more she thought about it, the better she liked the idea. Fill the empty hours. Give back a little to God. "Maybe I'll do that."

The waitress set the bill down in passing. Jessica reached for the plastic tray as Rob did, and they sat there in a ridiculous tug-of-war. They both laughed.

"Let's split it, okay?" Jessica pulled dollars from her purse.

"Okay," he said, placing his portion on the tray. "Next time you can buy," he added.

"Yeah, right." She was able to joke again. Ready to push out from under the heavy blanket of fear.

"I'm just teasing you." Rob grinned.

"I figured that."

"Thanks for joining me. It was a nice surprise. I'll see you on Tuesday night, then?"

"Same time, same channel," she said, keys in her hand, opening the door to a day that had brightened immeasurably since the dark hour she had left her apartment.

CHAPTER TWENTY-FOUR

Lawrence poured the Glenlivet over ice into crystal tumblers and handed one to Rob. "That movie stank," he said. "Especially the soundtrack. It was too bloody loud."

Lawrence rued the choice of a barbaric action flick on their one night out; his ears were still ringing. He hoped it wouldn't affect his music, not that he had written any lately. He settled into Rob's comfortable couch.

"You're getting old, Lawrence. Next time wear earplugs. You should thank me for getting you out of the rectory." Rob tasted his drink and grimaced, but licked his lips. "Oh, that's good." He sat in his recliner and flipped up the footrest.

"I needed a break," said Lawrence. "I'm going out of my mind there, I swear. If you read headlines about a bloody murder in the rectory, don't be surprised." He sipped his own drink, letting the icy amber liquid play on his tongue. The peaty aroma penetrated his senses. It was good scotch, but Lawrence could hardly appreciate it.

"Therese is driving me up the bloody wall, Rob, I tell you. I'm not exaggerating. And she knows it. She relishes it. She waits just until I'm about to work, then she knocks to ask me something inane, like have I eaten her tofu chips or used the last of her vitamin K. She ragged me about leaving the toilet seat up in the front bathroom—Rob, I don't even use that one! Just stupid stuff like that. She's the roommate from hell, and she doesn't even live there. Tom just lets her hang out, even when there's nothing to do." He sipped, feeling the golden trail burn down his throat.

"They got a movie tonight, *Free Tibetan Whales*, or some bleeding-heart sob story. They were in the living room watching it together when I left."

"Eating tofu chips, no doubt."

"I'm sure." Lawrence downed the last of his drink. He poured himself another, and offered the bottle to Rob.

Rob shook his head. "Still working on this one. Slow down, huh?"

"I don't care tonight. I can always sleep here, right?"

"Sure, if you need to."

"I've had it with that place." Lawrence let his frustration flow. "Now I can't even work. I'm blocked, Rob, totally blocked. I can't get past the *Sanctus*. I have less than three months left to finish this and record the demo, or that's it; I'll lose the chance of a lifetime." He took a long sip of scotch and swallowed. It didn't burn any longer. "I'm not going to make it, Rob. I can't take that woman any more. She's fucked with me one too many times."

"Maybe you're taking it too personally. It sounds like she's just a control freak. It probably has nothing to do with you." Rob's voice was soothing.

"Maybe. But it sure feels personal to me." Lawrence could feel the knot of stress in his chest beginning to dissolve with his second drink. "Being around her so much makes me so glad I'm queer."

Lawrence leaned back into the couch and closed his eyes. The aborted strains of his *Sanctus* clambered up the slope: *Sanctus, Sanctus, Sanctus*—there it stopped. He couldn't get past that line, that word. No music brimmed in his mind. He wanted nothing but peace in his rectory, just a few weeks, or even days, when he could finish the score. But all he could see was Therese, like a cloud blocking the light. All he could hear was her, not the music.

"Are you awake?" Rob's voice brought him back.

"Yeah." Lawrence opened his eyes and looked over at Rob. "I'm just wallowing here. Don't mind me."

It occurred to him that Rob had been fairly quiet all evening, and he remembered that Rob had seemed rather detached in recent days. He hadn't shared any gossip or griped at all. Lawrence sat up and leaned his elbows on his knees.

"What's up with you? You haven't said much lately. Is something wrong?"

Rob pursed his lips and shook his head. Then he flipped the lever on the recliner, and got to his feet. "I don't know. Maybe."

Lawrence felt a pang of contrition. "Want to talk about it?"

Rob walked to the window. Outside, the dark was riven by street lamps and the passing lights of cars. He stood with his back to Lawrence. "I've had something on my mind lately. I just want to—I don't know, say it out loud. See how it sounds. See if it makes sense."

"Let's hear it," said Lawrence.

"There's a woman—" Rob stopped.

The knot in Lawrence's chest clamped again. "Jesus Christ, Rob. A *fish*? Haven't you gotten that out of your system yet?"

Rob turned around, his eyebrows raised. "Excuse me? I believe I was trying to tell you something. I believe you asked me to share this?"

But Lawrence was livid. "Have you forgotten the Eleventh Commandment—'Thou shalt not fuck the flock?'"

"I haven't even said—"

"You don't have to. I've heard it before. Don't tell me—you're thinking of leaving."

"No, for God's sake, will you listen to me? Give me a break here, Lawrence. I listened to all your problems!"

"All right, all right." Lawrence was being a jerk, he knew it, but he had no stomach for woman trouble. Not now. Not tonight. He leaned back and crossed his arms. "Go on—you were saying? There's a woman?"

Rob took a deep breath and started again. "You know how I've been leading RCIA? Well, there's this woman in the group." He glanced at Lawrence, but Lawrence kept his mouth shut.

"She's been through a hard time. A horrible time. I confessed her. You know what it's like, hearing someone's confession, a really intense one? We've become close, sort of, somehow."

"Intimate, you mean?"

"In our conversations, yes. Nothing more."

"That's a *false* sense of intimacy, Rob. Every therapist knows that one. You must have missed Psych class that day. So you're in love with her now, I suppose?" He couldn't stand this happening to Rob—not again.

"No. I don't know. It's a feeling I have."

"Yeah, between your legs."

"Come on, Lawrence. This is different."

"Oh, please." Lawrence held up a hand to stop him. "Don't say it—please don't tell me she's *special*. I can't take it."

"Well, she is."

"Rob, why is it that you always end up with a woman? What is it that you can't live without, anyway? Or need I ask?"

"First of all, as you well know, I've had only one serious romance in my whole life, with Shannon. I left the seminary, it wasn't right for me, it didn't work out, and I came back.

"Second, I have never, ever cheated since ordination, which, by the way, is something *you* can't say. And third, I asked you to listen to me and hear me out. You won't even let me tell you. You've condemned me already. Thanks a lot."

Lawrence heard the hurt in Rob's voice. But he felt he must stop this madness of Rob's. He couldn't let his friend fall into the arms of some woman. Not when he needed him so much.

"Rob, you knew what you were getting into when we were ordained. This shouldn't come as a surprise." He made his voice calm, reasonable. "We all get lonely. It's part of the package. That's why we have these support groups, so we can lean on each other. I'm sorry I snapped at you. I'm here for you."

Rob looked at Lawrence a minute before speaking. Rob's voice was soft now, questioning. "All I'm saying is that I've met someone who made me stop and think. I haven't said anything to her about it; I haven't dated her, kissed her, nothing. There's no relationship." He turned to the window again. "In a way, it has nothing to do with *her*. But there's something working inside *me*. She's tapped something in me that I thought I never needed. I thought I'd put it to rest. I didn't think it mattered anymore. And suddenly it does." He looked back at Lawrence. "I'm not leaving. I'm just thinking. That's all."

"So what did you tell the Bishop about the Tribunal job?"

"I told him no, twice already. The personnel board asked again. I don't want to go to Rome, or to D.C. I want to be here, in a parish. And I don't want you to be such an ass. I just wanted to hear your honest opinion, your best advice." Rob rubbed his hand through his hair. "You're my best friend, my brother, Lawrence. I need you."

Lawrence was deeply touched. He wished he could say what Rob wanted to hear. But in his heart he didn't think Rob could withstand the temptation. If some girl came along and batted her eyes, Rob might jump ship. He wanted to make the best choice for Rob, and give advice Rob would appreciate in the long run.

"My best advice. You want my advice?" He stroked his chin, rubbing his fingers against the blond stubble. "It seems to me that you're weakest here in the parish. I suggest you take the Tribunal job and go with it. It puts you in line for the throne, Rob, you do realize that? Make some connections in Rome, work your way up the Tribunal, sit on a few committees, and in about twenty years you could be the Bishop, milord."

"I don't think so." Rob cracked an incredulous smile.

"Well, maybe not Bishop. But you could, you most certainly could head the Tribunal. That has its advantages, you have to admit." The balance was swaying, Lawrence could tell. The potential for advancement was tempting, even for Rob.

"You really, honestly, think so?"

"It could happen. It's too good an opportunity for you to miss. No one's offering it to me, you'll notice. There may be fags in the palace, but I haven't blown the right one yet."

Rob laughed in spite of himself. "Obviously."

"No, I'll have to stay here and rot with the Wicked Bitch of the West. Forever, I'm sure." Lawrence got up and poured both of them another drink. "Take the post, Rob. Get out of this rectory, get away from her, and just go. You'll be glad you did." He handed the drink back to Rob.

"Yeah, someday I'll thank you for this, huh?"

Lawrence smiled, glad to get back on normal footing again. They clinked glasses. "Just remember me when you come into your kingdom, Master."

CHAPTER TWENTY-FIVE

He saw her everywhere.

On Tuesday night, Jessica helped Caroline serve refreshments after RCIA. Rob overheard their conversation.

"You don't have to help me out, honey. You've got enough to do just getting ready for your baptism."

"I know. That's why I want to help. It makes me feel like part of the community."

On Wednesday night Rob opened the door of the room where the choir practiced. He needed to ask the choir director something, but he forgot what it was when he saw Jessica in the second row, soprano side, with her black binder full of next Sunday's hymns. She grinned at him. He had to leave and come back again when he remembered what he'd meant to ask. The choir's song stuck in his head the rest of the evening.

My love for you is an everlasting love;
I have called you, now you are Mine.

On Saturday mornings, the St. Vincent de Paul Society collected used clothing and toys and household objects. Rob came outside after saying the funeral of Mr. Dunleavy, and there was Jessica across the parking lot, bent over a pile of boxes and bags, sorting clothing. He spoke quietly with the mourners and embraced the Dunleavy grandchildren. As the mourners got into their cars to head out to Holy Sepulcher, Rob walked around to his

Jeep at the side of the rectory. He drove slowly by the St. Vinnie's workers and rolled down his window.

"Working hard?"

"Hardly working," Jessica called, waving. Her hair was pinned on top of her head like a mop, and her jeans and man's shirt were grubby. She smiled with an easy grace, and looked as if she were having fun.

Rob saw her laugh with another parishioner in his rear view mirror as he left the parking lot for the cemetery.

On Sunday morning Rob thought he saw her at the nine o'clock Mass but she seemed in a hurry, and he wasn't able to greet her. After Mass, the woman who ran the babysitting co-op stopped in at the rectory.

"Hey, thanks for sending us a warm body."

"A what?"

"You sent a volunteer to the co-op, right? Jessica something-or-other. A single gal. She's so good with the babies. She just jumped right in to help."

"Oh, Jessica. She's helping out at the co-op?" Rob laughed. "Oh, my."

"Why do you say that?"

"There's no zealot like a convert. She's in RCIA. She's going to be baptized at the Vigil. I suggested that she volunteer around the parish, and, my Lord, has she ever."

"Maybe you should suggest that to a few others. We could use the help."

When Rob went back to the church again to say the 10:30 Mass, there she was, in the choir, second row, soprano side.

My love for you is an everlasting love;
I have called you, now you are Mine.

He caught up with her after Mass, outside in the thin sunshine of early spring. "Hey, was that you I saw in the choir this morning?"

"Who, me? Couldn't have been!" Jessica hid her choir binder behind her back.

"Yes, you, the human blur. Busy, busy! When you take advice, you really take advice!"

"It was good advice, I guess." Her face lit with a smile. "But I love it. I'm having a great time. Thank you for suggesting it."

Rob saw such a difference, the tilt of her head, her quirky smile. Alive, he thought, awakened from her slumber, out from the veil she'd hidden behind for so long.

She checked her watch. "I have to run. I'm going to a lady's house this afternoon for a meeting. We're going to make quilts for the Holy Family Crisis Nursery." She fluttered away. "See you."

Rob watched her hurry to her car and drive out, waving again as she passed the church. He felt a little left behind.

He went back into the church to hang up his funeral vestments. Then he drifted into the rectory for the long solitude of a Sunday afternoon. He opened the newspaper and spread it out across the kitchen table while a fresh pot of coffee brewed. He picked out the book section just to scan the bestseller list, when a book review caught his attention, as Catholic items always did. Then he saw who had written the review.

Rob poured himself a cup of the scalding coffee.

Ordination, Not Subordination
By M. Patrice DuLac, SHS
Reviewed by Therese Fallon, CS

Syster Marie Patrice DuLac's manifesto on the ordination of women reads like a veritable laundry list of wrongs that the Roman Catholic Church has committed, intentionally or unintentionally, against women over the past two millennia. In fact, DuLac's tone bears full-fledged misanthropy. But why not? The misogynist, male-dominated Church has indeed failed to give women the same opportunities as men.

DuLac imbues her text with a clarity of argument and passion for her thesis—that celibacy should be optional, that women should be ordained, that there is nothing in gender or sex that prohibits us from serving God.
Women should be allowed to be priests, she argues, and frankly, it's about time...

Rob picked up the phone to call Lawrence. And just wait till the Bishop reads this, he thought.

CHAPTER TWENTY-SIX

❀

Cesar noticed an odd undercurrent in the diocesan office that afternoon. He felt it like a deep hum just beyond his range of hearing, or a whiff of the forbidden, and popped his head through the door to see what was happening. Down the long hall toward the Bishop's chambers, Cesar saw a priest walking purposefully, and two others tête-à-tête in the hall.

He sidled out of his office and up to the two in the hall, catching the words, "Now the shit hits the fan!"

"What's this?" Cesar closed in, wide-eyed.

The two priests exchanged glances, and one made a wry face. "You may as well tell him."

The other one beckoned. He leaned his face close to Cesar's. Cesar could smell garlic on the man's breath. "Patrick Keegan left." His tone clearly showed his thoughts on the topic.

"He fathered a child, you know," the first priest whispered, glancing toward the Bishop's office.

"Do you mean he left for good? Or just a leave of absence?" Cesar kept his voice low. It wouldn't do to be heard gossiping.

"Gone for good, I guess. Bishop got a letter in the mail today."

"A Dear John letter!" The two priests snickered.

"How's he taking it?"

"About the same as always—he's furious. Ready to crush any sign of infidelity under his iron thumb."

"Oh, well, then I'd better get back to work," Cesar said, pretending to cower. He put his fingers to his lips and winked at the priests, then slipped back into his office and shut the door.

Now. Whom should he call first?

No one answered at St. Justin or Resurrection. Cesar put the phone down and flipped his diocesan phone directory to William Fairlie's parish, St. Perpetua. Now there was someone who would appreciate a bit of news.

"St. Perpetua." Cesar knew it was William by his proper Latin pronunciation: *Pair-pet-oo-ah*.

"William, it is Cesar."

"Hail, Caesar," William said. "How are you, dear?"

"Just fine, thank you." Cesar gripped the receiver. "William, are you sitting down?"

"Oh, yes! Is it juicy?"

"Bishop had a letter today."

"Oooh, a letter? Tell, tell!"

"A Dear John."

"Go on. From?"

Cesar paused to let the suspense build.

"Cesar!"

"From Patrick." Cesar cupped his hand over his mouth to cover a giggle as William shrieked over the line.

"Noooo, tell me all!"

Cesar repeated what he'd heard, as William prompted him.

"So he's really gone, huh? Did he marry her yet?"

"I do not know. I will see what I can find out." Cesar wished he knew that bit already. "Poor boy, he has gone the way of the woman."

"There seems to be a rash of that going around," William said.

"What do you know?"

"Shall I torment you now?" William laughed evilly. "No, not this time. Well, now, guess who I saw having an intimate brunch with a fish the other day? In a cozy little nook downtown? Very cozy, I hasten to add."

"I do not know. Who?"

William wouldn't give it up so easily. "I was driving down Dolores and stopped at a light. You know how you just glance around when you're waiting at a long light? I thought I saw—a certain someone's vehicle. And I looked in the window and there he was. *Cum femina*. Can you guess?"

"Just tell me."

"Robert Souza. I swear to God."

Cesar felt a tingle of pleasure ripple down to his toes. What a day this was turning out to be.

"So now what do we do, Father?" William asked, his voice a whisper of confidence.

"Simple," Cesar said. "We confront him."

CHAPTER TWENTY-SEVEN

William set the tray of Brie and seeded crackers on the coffee table of the St. Perpetua rectory. The scents of garlic, lemon and dill wafted from William's kitchen out to the living room where the priests sat. A whole salmon was baking in the oven, while a salad waited on the sideboard to be dressed, and wine chilled in the refrigerator.

"Enjoy, gentlemen," William said, waving with a flourish worthy of a showgirl. He proceeded around the room with a bottle of Napa Chenin Blanc, refilling glasses.

Rob relaxed into the contours of the sofa and tasted his wine. "Yes, boys, enjoy this while you can, for Holy Week approacheth," he remarked, to groans.

"You mean Hell Week."

"Don't remind me."

Holy Week, the week preceding Easter, was notoriously stressful for the priests. There were a myriad of preparations to complete, from flowers and foot washing on Holy Thursday to stripping the church utterly bare before Friday, then redecorating with banners and more flowers for Holy Saturday and Easter. Rob's catechumens were excited and nervous about their impending initiation, and he knew he had a tense and frantic week ahead. And somehow, something horrible always happened during Holy Week. One year a beloved priest friend had dropped dead. Another year his mother had taken ill and he'd spent the week dashing back and forth between her hospital bed and his church duties. Everyone had war stories to tell of the Holy Week from hell, and Rob awaited the coming week with a mixture of anticipation and foreboding.

Lawrence walked in just then, and the men greeted him. He responded cheerfully, but to Rob, it seemed like a put-on. He didn't look as if he'd slept much lately. William pressed a wine glass into Lawrence's hand, and Phil moved over on the sofa.

"Have some, Lawrence." Phil cut deep into the Brie and smeared it on a cracker. "There's no meat in it," he cracked.

"That's right, Lawrence. Nothing like a vegetarian meal to build your strength!" William added.

"Tell that to Therese," Phil said, laughing.

"Don't even say her name. I'm on my day off!" Lawrence sank into an armchair.

"Don't tell me you're afraid of a nun!" Hector frowned. "Be a man. Show her who is in charge!"

"Easy for you to say." William watched Phil scrape at the beautiful cheese. "I notice you don't have a single nun in your parish. What did you do, Hector—scare them away, you macho man?"

"He had them burned at the stake. For wearing trousers," Cesar said. "That is what happened to Joan of Arc."

"What an exit—she went butch!" William laughed. "But, really, Lawrence, how is dear Sister Trayz?" He mimicked Therese's pronunciation.

"Don't ask." Lawrence waved the subject away. "Did anybody see the Pope on TV last night?"

"God, he looked ill!"

"This could be it, you know. He's not getting any younger."

The talk eddied and swelled, laughter and conversation both loud and soft.

Lawrence got up, giving Rob a significant glance, and Rob followed him to the wet bar. "I have to talk to you," Lawrence said in a low voice.

"It's not going well?"

"It's not going at all. I'm still blocked. She's making me crazy. I can't eat, I can't work, I can't even sleep anymore. I called Dave Porter on the personnel board and begged for a transfer, but he says they're in the middle of some other crisis right now and I'll have to wait."

Lawrence's face was pale and shadowed, and for the first time, Rob noticed the deep lines around his blue eyes, and a crease in his forehead that he hadn't seen there before.

"They mean Patrick," Rob said. "And that nun's book is stirring up a hornet's nest, too."

Lawrence shook his head. "I don't care what they mean. I can't stand it. I'm serious. I have this huge deadline looming. I have to meet it or no contract, no CD, no nothing." His voice trembled. "I'm losing it."

"What if you ask for a temporary leave? Come stay at my place and finish the work."

"I don't know. The music room is perfect—or it would be, if she weren't there. It's all set up with my recording stuff. I wish she would just drop dead. I'm at the end of my rope here, Rob."

"Well, hang on. We'll think of something."

William cleared his throat. "*Messieurs, le diner.*" He had arranged the table with care, three forks, two spoons, two knives at every place; the antique refectory table was covered with a pewter-gray damask cloth, napkins folded into mitres. Before each place was a small silver vase with a pale lilac rose and a spray of baby's breath.

The men gathered around the table to bless the food. William said, "Loving God, You unite us with our friends and nourish us with Your bounty in this Lenten season. We ask that You bless us and Your gifts, and all those who hunger and thirst, and we ask this, as always, through Christ our Lord."

"Amen," six voices strong.

At dinner Rob noticed Cesar and William exchanging glances and mouthing words to each other. Phil ate with his usual gusto. Hector ate just a few bites of the fish and a plain baked potato, and had brought a chamomile tea bag for after supper, "to settle my stomach," he said, defensively. Lawrence was moody and said little.

Rob got up to help William clear plates afterward. Cesar followed them into the kitchen. The door swung shut.

"Good dinner, Willie," Rob said. "Can I help you make coffee or something?"

"Actually, Robert, you *can* help me with something," William said, taking the dome off a home-baked cheesecake on a crystal cake stand. "You can help me with a puzzle." William sliced the dessert as he spoke, his gaze lowered, intent on his task. A smile played at his lips.

"A puzzle." Rob looked at William, slicing cheesecake, and Cesar, who smirked in the corner. "What kind of puzzle?"

The other two priests glanced at each other. "Well, I was wondering who you're dating?"

"I'm not dating anyone."

"Not even someone with red hair?" William raised his eyebrows.

"Do you often have brunch dates?" Cesar added.

"Oh, that."

"Oh!" Cesar laughed. "So it is true."

"What's true? That I ate breakfast with a parishioner?"

"She is a parishioner?"

"Come on, you guys. It was nothing, just a spur of the moment—"

"Sperm of the moment, he means." William laughed.

"You guys are pathetic." He almost laughed at the inanity. "Make some coffee, huh?" Rob walked back to the dining room and sat down again.

"What's going on?" Phil asked.

"Nothing," Rob said as Cesar and William returned with plates of cheesecake.

"Love is many splendored thing," William sang, and added, "Roberto has a case of Patrick-itis."

"I do not." Rob folded his napkin, his face flushing warm from the wine and the heat of the room.

Lawrence turned to look at Rob. "My God, you're blushing."

"I am not."

"Are you gettin' some, Rob?" Phil cackled.

"No!"

"She's a redhead, I heard. Is she a redhead *all over?*"

"Shut up!" Rob balled his fists in his lap. "I told you already, there's nothing going on." He looked around the table at his laughing friends, hopeless. "You don't believe me."

"Is that the official story? Or the official denial?"

"Excuse me," Rob said. He pushed back the chair and walked into the kitchen. They were impossible, so adolescent, and unstoppable. No matter what he said, they twisted it. He used to think that was funny.

Rob stood at the sink and looked out the window. But the world was black outside, and all he could see was the green and white kitchen in the glass, his own reflection, an angry man, alone. Behind him in the reflection, he saw Lawrence come in.

"Rob, you okay?"

"I'm fine." Rob turned around and faced Lawrence.

"Well, what *is* going on?" Lawrence asked. "Didn't we already decide that you're taking the Tribunal job?"

"I turned it down."

"What? I thought you knew what was best. You were going to get away from her."

"No, I never said that. You said that. I said I want to be in a parish with the people, and when the personnel board called me last week, I turned them down. It's not a job I want. I don't want to go to Rome."

"You mean you want to be with her."

"There's no *her* to get away from. I'm not involved."

"Yet."

"Jesus, doesn't anybody listen? I said I'm not—" Rob stopped. "Just forget it."

"You know what, Rob?" Lawrence shook his head slowly, as if he pitied Rob. "You're lying to everybody, and the saddest thing is, you're lying to yourself. You have the look. You're in love with that woman. Haven't you learned anything?"

"Thank you for your support." Rob walked out of the kitchen into the dining room where the talk ceased as he entered. He stopped to pick up his jacket from the back of the sofa. "Thanks for dinner. I'll see you." He left, pulling the door shut behind him, knowing that the talk raged on. He might as well have poured gasoline on a fire.

Holy Week

CHAPTER TWENTY-EIGHT

Lawrence traced a gentle *glissade* up the white keys of the piano. As he had said to Rob at William's dinner party, things had not been going well. And now they were worse.

He had argued with Rob, and after Rob left, the teasing grew ever merciless. Lawrence couldn't bear to hear it anymore; the innuendo had lost its humor to him. More than ever before, Lawrence was seized with the very likely reality that Rob might leave. His best friend in this world might step outside the ring and go another way. The other priests had continued to joke, but Lawrence claimed exhaustion and left.

The next morning, Lawrence phoned Rob. Rob answered, but his tone cooled when he heard Lawrence's voice.

"Rob, I'm sorry about last night. Things got out of hand. We went too far."

"And?"

"And we shouldn't have teased you."

Lawrence didn't know what else to say. He held the silent receiver to his ear and ran lines through his mind; nothing seemed suitable. *I hope you're happy together. Is she worth it? Whatever you do, just don't get her pregnant.*

Rob sighed impatiently. "I appreciate that, Lawrence. But frankly, that's not a problem for me. I'm a big boy. I can handle a little ribbing."

If things were all right between them, Lawrence would have jumped in and joked about condoms with ribbing, or made a boner joke. But he couldn't now.

"The problem is that you—that none of you—believe me when I say I'm not involved with her, or with anyone. And you called me a liar. In front of everyone. You're my best friend, and you're supposed to know me. So why don't you believe me?"

"Oh, c'mon, Rob. Why do you think? You just came to me a few weeks ago, crying over this woman. And now that I think about it, I saw you two talking at the Rite of Election, and then William saw you two on a date—in public, for God's sake. You're hooked."

"That's not true."

"Oh, don't give me the denial. I already heard that sorry song from Patrick. We've gone through this before, don't you remember? 'Aren't you happy for me, Lawrence?' Yeah, I'm ecstatic. I'm jumping for joy, watching you dive in again, throw away your education, your career, your future, your *everything* on a goddamned fish."

"For the last time, I'm telling you. There is nothing going on."

"Rob, I'm sorry." Lawrence couldn't stand to argue anymore. "I've just been through this with you before, and I hate to see it tear you up again. I hate to see you hurt again."

"Then try listening to what I'm saying." Lawrence heard a voice behind Rob through the phone, Rob's hand muffling his response. Rob came back to the line. "My appointment's here." His voice was curt. "I'll talk to you later."

Lawrence tried again later but got no response. He called several times, and finally left a message, trying to joke, to make it light. "Don't rush into anything! Call me first!"

He pressed the piano keys, a quick climb into Debussy, melding into Satie, too light, darkened the melody into Chopin, major, minor, down into his childhood *Saints* again, helpless, hopeless St. Jude.

A priest like Lawrence needed a friend, someone to laugh with, hear his confession, share the inside joke, the bitterness when the reality of vocation got a little too harsh. A friend like Rob made the loneliness easier to bear. They were touchstones in each other's lives. Lawrence always called Rob first with good news, with gossip, with a bitch and moan on his darker days. Rob had always called Lawrence first, too. After decrepit old Monsignor Finley died, when it suddenly became evident that Rob would be first of their ordination class to become a pastor, Rob and Lawrence had whooped at each other on the phone. And when the day actually came, Lawrence was there to concelebrate as the Bishop installed Rob as pastor of St. Justin.

Rob had heard almost every confession Lawrence had made since they were ordained six years before. He knew every detail of every sin that charged Lawrence's heart. Well, almost everything.

But Rob hadn't confessed to Lawrence in a long time, and somehow Lawrence doubted that there was nothing to confess. With the inner certitude of a brother, of a lover, Lawrence knew Rob's heart had strayed. There was a shadow between them now, in the shape of a woman. Lawrence felt bruised and cheated.

So now the denials. Now the adamant, "I swear to God," right on the heels of his plaintive, "But this is different." What next? Sneaking around, late night visits. Gravel crunching in the driveway at dawn. The woman's face at Mass, expectant, possessive, nodding at the words of the homily that were meant especially for her. An almost sexual exchange in the giving and receiving of Communion. He had seen it before. He wouldn't stand back and watch it happen again.

After the weekend, still exhausted from the lengthy Masses for Passion Sunday, Lawrence took the collection money to the bank to deposit. First he had to stand in a long line, then wait while a particularly stupid teller counted the rolls of coins, exclaimed over the two-dollar bills that some chump had thrown in the basket, and generally made a fool of herself flirting with Lawrence. He was not in the mood. Finally he got out of there and, since he was in the neighborhood, he drove over to St. Justin Martyr. He meant to take Rob out for lunch as a peace offering, to break the ice between them again.

But as Lawrence sat there in his car, waiting for traffic to pass so he could turn into the church's parking lot, he saw the chestnut-haired woman come out of the rectory, smiling over her shoulder at Rob behind her, just the two, no one else, and followed her to her car. She got in and closed the door, put the window down, and Rob threw back his head and laughed. Then Rob leaned over and maybe kissed her, he thought, he couldn't really see, couldn't sit there and watch.

Lawrence put his foot on the gas and drove away, back to Resurrection.

St. Justin Martyr wasn't neutral territory anymore. It was unwise for Rob to stay there. Lawrence could see that even if Rob couldn't. He knew what the depth of Rob's anger would be when he found out, but what else remained? There was only one thing Lawrence could do.

In his room, he dialed the number with a shaking finger, his heart full of regret, and listened to the ring, a treble pulse, B flat.

CHAPTER TWENTY-NINE

Rob checked himself again in the mirror before he left. He looked priestly enough. His long-sleeved clerical was fresh from the cleaners. He buttoned the tight top button at his neck, choking a bit, and slipped his collar, stiff and white, into the tabs at his throat. Gleaming like a baby's tooth, the white square showed against the black shirt and the brown neck. His black pants were pressed to a knife crease, his black leather shoes glossy from the polishing cloth. Lawrence would have approved and made a joke about the shoes matching his purse, but Rob shook the thought away, still hurt and angry at his friends.

A message was waiting on his answering machine when Rob had returned from an Easter-planning meeting Tuesday: "The Bishop wants to see you on Wednesday at 2 p.m." Some invitations cannot be declined.

That night, Rob led the RCIA group through a guided meditation, telling the catechumens to relax and let go of all anxiety. He avoided any prolonged glance or conversation with Jessica and knew she noticed. His stomach was in knots, dreading the next day's interview.

The squat brick building which housed the diocesan offices and the Bishop's office sat on a main thoroughfare in the next town, busy as any other office building, except for the number of priests and nuns going in and out. Before the building lay a large courtyard with stone benches and flowering plum trees. A fountain splashed to one side, and a statue of Mary graced the other. Shrubs and flowers brightened the cement planters.

Inside the diocesan offices, marriages were annulled, dispensations were granted, and vocations were pledged. The Bishop in his office engaged in correspondence with other bishops in the state, the U.S. Conference of Bishops, and Rome. He spoke to the press, presided at the cathedral, and handled private disciplinary matters of the clergy. He played a decent round of golf with the Congressman and the mayor on Tuesdays.

Rob found street parking, fed the meter, and went inside. He saw a couple of priests he knew and nodded to them. The dark red carpet cushioned footsteps; Rob, with the same feeling of consequence he always felt when he saw the prelate, took the carpeted stairs up to the second floor, where the Reverend Bishop Paul Cornelius kept his suite of offices.

Rob passed Cesar's office on his way to the Bishop's suite. He didn't stop or look, although the door was open. He saw a black blur—Cesar in clericals, and heard the man gasp as he passed, a whispered, "Robert, wait." Rob walked on down the long hall, the walls of which were hung with large framed photographs: the Pope and the Bishop standing together, the Bishop blessing the Pascal candle, the Bishop's own ordination long ago.

Cesar popped out of his office into the hall behind him. Rob didn't turn his head but knew, as well as he had ever known that scrawny Filipino boy from Bambang, knew that the man followed a discreet step behind.

"Robert, Robert, where are you going?" The whisper was a plea.

Rob stopped at the secretary's desk, but he was expected, waved on, and Rob went into the Bishop's office. Behind him, as Rob turned to shut the door, he saw Cesar, his mouth an O of shock, his eyes wide and white. The door closed with a pneumatic click.

"Hello, Rob." The Bishop greeted him from his high-backed chair behind the large desk. "Come, sit down." He set down his pen and slipped the papers he was writing into a folder. The Bishop's black-framed bifocal glasses were perched on the end of his rather thin nose. He extended a venous hand. Rob shook it.

"Thank you, Bishop." Rob sat in the armless chair that faced the desk.

The Bishop folded his hands and leaned his chin on them. "How's it going, Rob? Are you getting along all right?"

"I'm well, thank you." He felt like a child, waiting for the slap.

"Everything all right at St. Justin?"

"Fine, just fine."

"I saw that your collection has gone up again this year. You must be doing something right. What's the secret, eh, short homilies? Doughnuts after Mass?" The Bishop gave a dry laugh.

"I guess they like me." Rob tried a wan smile.

"Is that so?" The Bishop looked long at Rob. "What's going on, Father Souza?"

"I'm not sure I know." Rob wanted to laugh suddenly, bad boy in the principal's office. He bit his cheek instead.

"There's a woman." It wasn't a question, but a statement of fact.

Rob's fingers curled into his palms.

"That woman from St. Justin who spoke to me at the cathedral, during the Rite of Election—she seemed particularly attached to you. Is it she?"

Rob closed his eyes. *Oh, Jessica.*

"Well?"

"Well, what do you want me to say?" He looked helplessly at the Bishop. "If I deny it, you won't believe me. Even my best friends don't believe me. But—oh, never mind." Rob couldn't argue anymore. He felt a peculiar sense of destiny, that no matter what he said, his fate was already out of his hands and decided.

Everything he felt toward Jessica seemed tangled in an impossible knot. He had dreamed of her, and then shunted it aside; he sensed her presence like an echo as she crossed the church, then quelled his thoughts. Every time he felt the rush, the full spout of his longing, he crushed it, made himself ignore it, forget her, remember the rules, his promises, the obligations of his call. And still it lingered, traces of her, images that replayed in his mind. The stroke of her hand on St. Margaret's marble base. Her fingertips, wet with holy water, tracing the Sign of the Cross on her forehead, breast, petite shoulders left and right. The kiss of peace on a Sunday. Her naked, anguished heart. Himself, a priest. It was hopeless, he could see.

"Well, let's just say once bitten, twice shy, eh?" The Bishop pushed at his glasses. "Your friend Father Keegan really bit it deep, didn't he? It does nothing for our public relations, as I'm sure you're aware."

"I'm not Patrick."

The Bishop sat for a moment, rubbing a finger at the side of his nose. "You started to say something a minute ago. What was it?"

"Nothing."

"Nothing much, or nothing you can say to me?" The blue eyes seemed to pierce Rob's soul.

"Nothing I can even say to myself."

"I see." The Bishop swiveled his chair around to the credenza behind him. He pulled a file from the top basket and looked into it for some time, then set it back in the basket and turned around again.

"Rob, I've made a decision. You're going to come to work here in the canon law office. We'll get you the application for either Catholic U. or the Gregorian, you decide which, and you can go next year, get your canon law degree. But you're leaving St. Justin. It's better this way." The old man watched for Rob's reaction.

"Against my preference, you want me here?"

The Bishop nodded.

Rob couldn't decline. He had promised obedience to his Bishop, and he had always kept his promises. A wave of despair washed through him. Rob folded his hands in his lap, good Catholic boy. "When do I have to move? Can I at least get through Easter with my RCIA?"

"Of course. Let's say May 1. That gives you a month to pack and tie up the loose ends. You can move to Joan of Arc, fill in there on weekends, but you'll work here during the week."

Rob sat, tight-lipped, listening to the old man tear up the life around him, pull him from the people, from the parish, *from the woman*, from his life, and he thanked the Bishop, obedient priest that he was. "Thank you."

The Bishop shook his head. "I don't think so, Rob, no. You don't thank me now. Perhaps in time, eh? Go on, now. I'll see you in the office on that Monday, May 3. Come and knock on the door; we'll have lunch together."

Rob nodded and left the office. The long hall seemed endless. His mind was wheeling.

"Robert, wait." Cesar slipped into step beside him. "What happened? You look as pale as a ghost."

Rob wanted to get out, away from all these priests, the too-tight collar, the incestuous infighting among them all. And now Cesar, like a little brother, tagging along behind him, *c'mon, tell me.*

Rob looked over at Cesar and stopped. "What do you think happened? Don't you know already, Gladys?"

Cesar would have smiled at his old nickname, but Rob cowed him with a glance.

"I'm getting transferred from St. Justin into the chancery office. They're delivering me from evil. Are you all happy now?"

"Oh, Robert." Cesar looked shocked. "You have to go?"

"Obedience, remember? It's another promise I haven't broken." Rob started walking again. Something in Cesar's expression bothered him, though. "You had no idea this was coming?"

"I give you my word, I did not know." Cesar crossed himself. "I am so sorry, Robert. But— "

"What?"

"There was a phone call on Monday. I just heard rumors. I didn't know it was about you."

"Who called?" It had to be someone from Friday's dinner. Rob's eyes locked with Cesar's.

Cesar slowly shook his head, utter sympathy in his dark eyes.

"No." Rob felt he had been punched in the stomach. *My God, Lawrence, how could you?*

Triduum

CHAPTER THIRTY

Rob awoke Thursday morning with a pain in his head like a spring stretched taut. He had slept terribly; the glass of wine before bed had not helped, or not helped enough. He had twisted in the sheets, unable to find his ease, kicked off the blankets and pulled them back again, then settled at last into uneasy slumber. He dreamed of Lawrence and again Lawrence, his friend's mouth moving, the music too loud, Rob couldn't hear what he said. Rob lay in his bed and looked at the ceiling, too bright with the slanting rays of morning. He had lain in that bed and looked at that ceiling for hundreds of mornings, for six years, at smooth white plaster that was yet unsmooth, a world of small planes and shadows that curved above his head.

Rob massaged his temples and rolled from bed, stumbling toward the heat and jolt of coffee, losing himself in the ritual of the filter, the water, the number of scoops. He leaned against the counter in his shorts, his eyes closed painfully against the glare of day, while the coffeemaker snorted and mulled. Rob poured himself a cup before the maker had finished and got a mug silted with coffee grounds for his reward. He drank it anyway, a bitter brew with floaters.

It was Holy Thursday, a day he had looked forward to but now faced with glum determination. Beginning at sundown as in the tradition of their Jewish heritage, Holy Thursday marked the first of the three days of the Sacred Triduum: Holy Thursday, Good Friday, and Holy Saturday. Then came Easter itself, beginning with the Vigil on Saturday, on into Sunday. Three days of intense prayer, ceremony, tradition. Three Sulpician priests from the seminary coming in to help with the liturgies. Three days to culminate the journey toward initiation for his catechumens in RCIA. Lent and Easter far surpassed Christmas as the most stressful time of the church year. Most priests took much-needed vacation right after Easter. Rob would be packing boxes instead.

He went into his office and looked through his liturgical desk calendar. Each day, month by month, listed the religious feasts; the little chasuble symbol in the corner of each page reminded him what color vestments to wear, and left space to record his appointments, which he wrote only in pencil, as there were often cancellations. Rob found *May 3, Monday in the fifth week of Easter, vestment color white*, took a black pen and wrote in his neat block print, "Chancery Office, 9 a.m." He erased all of the events related to St. Justin Martyr after that. Someone else would finish the RCIA sessions on Tuesdays after Easter. Someone else would give the second graders their First Communion in May. Someone else would take Rob's place on the committees, at the altar, in his bed in the rectory. Another priest would move in. The world moved on.

In any other case, on any other day, Rob would have reached for the phone and called Lawrence, worked it out, come up with a plan of action. He knew Lawrence would commiserate, invite him for lunch or a movie, would have joked and lightened the mood, so that the grim future could be borne. Throughout the day, Rob found his hand reaching for the phone, once even held the receiver and began the memorized dance of the finger upon the keypad to call Lawrence. He stopped before he hit the final number, and pressed the button to quickly end the call. Lawrence's perfidy, on top of the false accusations of Friday night, wounded Rob to the marrow.

Still, the day hastened by. Under a haze that felt like a hangover, Rob made sure that everything was ready for Holy Thursday, the Mass of the Lord's Supper. The handbells to ring for the *Gloria*. The holy oils, consecrated by the Bishop at the Chrism Mass—Oil of the Sick, Oil of Catechumens, Sacred Chrism—in their cut-glass flasks etched with Latin initials, *OI, OC, SC,* to be presented in the processional that night. The Altar of Repose, which he set up in the chapel, draped with a thick brocade altar cloth. The flowers Rob had ordered from the florist, all in white— iris, lilies, tulips and narcissus—arrived and now stood in tall clear vases around the altar. He collected basins and towels for the ritual washing of feet. He set Luis, his seminarian from St. Joseph's, to fold programs. And he polished the gold-plated ciborium, in which the consecrated Hosts would rest on the altar after Mass, for the Veneration of the Body of Christ.

Too much to do, and the day flew, barely time for a frozen dinner in the microwave at six o'clock and a quick shave before Mass. At six-thirty, St. Justin Martyr was filling, and by seven, when the Mass began, it was full.

The young thurifer went first in the procession, sweet gray smoke wafting from the brass censer as she carried it. Another girl followed with the processional cross. Then came the lector with the Lectionary hoisted above his head, and three parishioners carrying the oils. Rob had selected a catechumen from RCIA to carry the Oil of Catechumens, and he had intentionally not chosen Jessica. The three Sulps from the seminary came next, and Rob followed, his pace measured and reverent, his eyes focused on the cross that hung behind the altar. And still he knew, like a breath on the back of his neck, when he passed her.

So began the Holy Thursday Mass, its prayer and liturgy around the story of the Last Supper and how Jesus knew that a loved one who dipped into the same dish would betray Him. The congregation heard the story of the washing of feet, how Jesus humbled Himself for His friends and gave His service to them. They heard the story of Jesus' commandment to His disciples to love. It was all there in the book, Scripture Rob had heard and studied his whole life, yet tonight every word seemed to resonate with new meaning:

I give you a new commandment; love one another as I have loved you...

The devil had already induced Judas, son of Simon Iscariot, to hand Jesus over...

You may not understand what I am doing, but later you will understand...

Rob rose from the presider's chair, took off his chasuble and handed it to one of the Sulps. He stepped down to the main floor and rolled up the sleeves of his alb. Twelve chairs had been placed at the front of the church with basins before them. Rob's seminarian, Luis, brought warm water in a large pitcher and filled the first basin. The choir began to sing quietly as two ushers brought forth twelve parishioners to the seats.

Lord, do you wash my feet?
If I do not, you can have no part with me.

Rob knelt before the first one to wash his foot. The man's foot was thin and knobby; Rob could feel bone and sinew as he washed gently. Luis handed him a soft towel. Rob bent to kiss the instep, and released the man's foot. An usher removed the basin and Luis filled the next one. Rob washed each foot, down the line on his knees, another man's flat foot with hairy toes; a baby's tiny foot, small enough to nestle into his hand; an old man's foot with calluses and crooked toes; a teenager's slender foot with blue-painted toenails and a hemp ankle bracelet.

The next foot was Jessica's; Rob had seen her come to the front but turned his mind to his work. He did not look up, unable to match the face with the feeling, not now. He knelt before her, cupped his damp hand under her naked foot and placed it into the warm, soapy water. He heard her intake of breath, saw her toes splay and curl at the water's surprising warmth.

Rob kept his head down, rubbed his fingers into the arch of her sole, massaging her tendons, reached up her ankle and drew his hand down the length of her foot, gently traced his finger under her toes. They flexed, pink, wet toes, and again he grasped and pressed firm into the arch, the taut tendons, and rubbed around the rosy heel. Luis handed him a towel; Rob placed it across his knees and brought her foot from the water to his lap.

Jessica's skin was warm, her toes wriggling slightly as he dried them. Rob lifted her foot from his lap, as reverently as at the Elevation of the Host, and pressed his mouth softly to her instep. He released her and moved before the next chair, and the next, until he had washed the feet of the twelve.

The choir finished its song as he rolled down his sleeves and pulled the chasuble back over his head.

Love one another as I have loved you.
As I have loved you.

CHAPTER THIRTY-ONE

Father Rob had asked his catechumens to try to stay home on Holy Saturday, if at all possible, to pray and prepare for the Vigil that night. Jessica rose early, put the kettle on for tea, and then prayed a little, while the water boiled. Every morning she took a little prayer book with her to read on the train to work; it gave her a clean start to the day. But at home, she prayed in her living room, near the little altar she had set up on a table, with her rosary, a candle, and a holy card with a picture of Our Lady of Sorrows that Father Rob had given her.

She made a piece of plain toast, but it was a day of fasting and preparation, so she didn't eat anything else. The day seemed strange to her, a day of anticipation, of longing. She drifted around her small apartment aimlessly, determined to keep the day holy, but uncertain how to do that. The gardeners came to clean up the apartment complex, their mowers and blowers roaring around the narrow strips of lawn, leaving behind silence and a sharp green scent of cut grass. Jessica saw children come out to play; young mothers sat in sunshine on benches around the courtyard and watched their little ones ride tricycles and pull wagons around and around. The sound of plastic wheels grating on concrete rumbled through the complex like a small thunderstorm.

At around eleven, the mailman came. Jessica watched the mothers clustered around the mailboxes, as if this were the peak of their uncomplicated day, and knew a ridiculous thrill of anticipation herself. She made herself wait until the small crowd dispersed, then she slowly walked out to check her mail: a postcard from an old friend, some bills, and a grocery store sale paper. Nothing to get excited about. She walked back to her apartment and closed the door.

Jessica observed the toddlers in the early April sun from her window. She knew that her child, if she had borne it, would have been four years old. What were four-year-olds like, she wondered. Did they go to preschool? She envisioned a little girl riding a pink tricycle, its wheels skimming the pavement, her thin red braids fluttering in the spring breeze. A small boy, on the floor with his tiny cars and trucks, making motor sounds with his tongue. Children of her dreams.

Her hands cradled her belly to protect what wasn't there. *I'm sorry, baby. I'm so sorry.* Jessica wanted to go outside and pick up one of the little ones, hold it close to her, just to feel what it was like to hold a child. *You knit me in my mother's womb,* said the Psalm. There was a someday child, a future baby in her life, she hoped; she prayed she wasn't damaged, sterile and cold inside. No more than she already was. It would be a just punishment.

But Father Rob had confessed her and absolved her sins. Clean of heart she went to her initiation this weekend. Never mind the shower dream. It was unconscious, uncontrolled fantasy. There was nothing real there. His smile was pure friendship, his interest paternal. No bond between them. No reason to hope for more.

In the evening, moonless and black with bright pinpoints of stars overhead, the catechumens gathered for the Easter Vigil in the dark courtyard outside of St. Justin Martyr. Parishioners drove into the parking lot and walked quietly to the courtyard, clustered around the low platform where the first part of the Vigil would take place. There seemed an injunction on noise; people spoke in hushed tones.

Jessica stood with the other catechumens near the platform, upon which waited an unlit brazier near two altar servers in their white surplices. Ushers passed small white candles around, to be lit after the blessing of the fire. When the crowd had overflowed the courtyard, and her watch showed eight o'clock, Father Rob, ghostlike in his white chasuble, walked slowly from the church and stepped up on the platform. He stood for a long moment like some Etruscan statue, his white vestments lent a reddish cast from the street lamps.

An altar girl stood before him, holding the Sacramentary and a tiny flashlight. Father Rob opened the book to the proper page, closed his eyes briefly, tightly, as if in pain. He took a deep breath, then opened his eyes and began to speak the invocation.

"Dear friends in Christ, on this most holy night, when our Lord Jesus Christ passed from the darkness of death to the light of new life, the Church invites her children throughout the world to come together for this journey, to make this vigil and prayer." His voice echoed in the courtyard.

Father Rob took a long match from an altar boy and lit the fire, holding the draped brocade of his chasuble back from the blaze. He extended a hand over the leaping flames, blessing them. "Make this fire holy and instill in us the flame of new hope." Then he blessed and lit the Paschal candle, from which the first small candles were lit. From hand to hand the light was passed, each tiny flame a child of the flame before it, each a grandchild of the greater Paschal flame, the blessed fire, until the faces in the courtyard flickered in the candlelight, and a golden aura curved above them.

Father Rob began the procession around the courtyard and into the darkened church, the catechumens falling in behind him, the rest of the parishioners further back. Three times he stopped the procession: at the door of St. Justin Martyr, halfway up the long center aisle, and when he reached the front; three times he sang out in his clear, deep voice, "Christ our Light."

"Thanks be to God."

As the parishioners filled the pews and lined the walls at the back and sides, the catechumens took their place of honor in the front row. Father Rob took his place at the ambo, his face golden in the flicker of candlelight. With a command, the people extinguished their candles, and in the semi-darkness, lit only by the few candles at the altar, Father Rob began to sing, *a capella*, the ancient text of the *Exultet*, the Easter hymn of joy.

Rejoice, heavenly powers. Sing, choirs of angels.

From darkness to light, sin to redemption, separation to unity, the Vigil went on.

Much later, after the long stories of Creation, Abraham's sacrifice, and the great Exodus, after the words of the prophets Isaiah, Baruch and Ezekiel, after the Gospel of the Resurrection, and Father Rob's homily, at last came time for the baptisms. Jessica could not stop trembling.

Her sponsor, Susan, squeezed her hand. "This is it!"

Jessica couldn't answer. The choir began to sing the *Litany of Saints*.

"St. Michael." The parishioners responded in song, *Pray for us*, after every name.

"St. John the Baptist." *Pray for us.*

"Saints Peter and Paul." *Pray for us.*

"St. Andrew." *Pray for us.*

The names washed over her, name after name, wave after wave, people who died for Christ, who died in Christ.

"St. Mary Magdalene." Even a prostitute was sainted. *Pray for us.*

"St. Stephen." The first martyr. *Pray for us.*

"St. Francis and St. Dominic." *Pray for us.*

"St. Theresa." The story of a soul. *Pray for us.*

"All holy men and women." *Pray for us.*

The chant went on and on, mesmerizing in its singsong, hypnotic repetition; she felt herself swaying slightly. Incense perfumed the church; the sanctuary, resonating with the words of the chant, glowed with candles. Father Rob seemed to float as he moved to stand behind the baptismal font, which spilled into a pool in a clear sheet of water.

When the last line of the chant died away, Father Rob put his hands into the water of the baptismal font, swirled them around and blessed the waters. The priest's swirling hands caused water to splash over the edge, out into the pool below it. The first catechumen stepped forward, his sponsors nearby. He stepped barefoot into the shallow pool and knelt in the water in his jeans and shirt. Father Rob took a pitcher and dipped it into the water. He poured it over the catechumen's head, "I baptize you in the name of the Father, and of the Son and of the Holy Spirit."

A huge cheer went up from the catechumens, and the congregation applauded. Dripping water from his hair, grinning, the catechumen stood and was helped from the pool, wrapped in towels and whisked away to change his clothes.

Jessica was next. She slipped her sandals from her feet, and stepped forward. Eyes on her, so many eyes. Trembling, she stepped into the pool, gasping from the touch of the water, unexpectedly warm. Jessica knelt in the clear water, her black cotton shift soaking up water, weighting her down as the priest scooped the pitcher around her. He was so near; she could see the numbers on his watch, the dark hair on his wrist inside the sleeve of the alb.

The holy water cascaded over her head, filling her eyes and ears, down her face and shoulders, ran down her back and between her breasts, and she heard screams and cheers and applause, and Father Rob's deep voice through it all, saying, "— and of the Son, and of the Holy Spirit." *All sin washed clean.* Jessica gasped for new breath. Tears poured down her wet face. She knelt in the warm water, felt chills ridge her skin, her hair curling in wet strands on her face and neck, her elbow grasped as he helped her up and gave her to her sponsor. Hands wrapped towels around her and helped her from the pool.

Later, the new Catholics formed a line across the front to receive their First Communion, their hands cupped like hungry children. As Father Rob pressed the consecrated wafer into the palm of the first catechumen, his voice said, "The Body of Christ," and the catechumen—no, the Catholic—said, "Amen."

He moved in front of Jessica, in dry clothes now, her hair still curling damply around her face. She raised her hands to receive.

In his eyes, with a glaze of tears, a look seemed to confess more than affection. There was something almost connubial in the act; he, the Bridegroom, she, the Bride, sharing the wedding feast. He presented the wafer like a gift, a pledge of something unimagined. Then she did imagine, she did go on, felt the cool slip of gold on her finger, took the first taste of her new life. Into her hand he pressed the broken wafer, a piece of his own Communion.

"The Body of Christ, Jessica."

"Amen."

He moved on, and another priest offered her the chalice. She sipped, and he, too, moved past.

She raised her eyes to gaze at the crucifix above their heads. She belonged. She was in. *Thank you.*

Afterward, the congregation poured from the church toward the reception. Father Rob and the new Catholics milled in the hospitality room, bright with lights and paper streamers and balloons. Caroline sliced pieces from a large white sheet cake bedecked with curly *Congratulations* and yellow icing roses. Harold poured Champagne. Parents and godparents, sponsors and friends filled the room, laughing and talking loudly.

Members of the choir gave Jessica a bouquet of blue and white irises, a silver necklace with a charm of the Holy Spirit dangling from it. Her sponsor, Susan, gave her a rosary and a little plaque to put on her desk at work. Parishioners, people she didn't even know, hugged her and congratulated her and shook her hand. *At last, I belong. At last, a place at the table.*

Someone put on a CD of Big Band hits and people began to dance. Jessica sipped her Champagne, bright bubbles in a plastic cup. All the images of the night seemed a tremendous blur to her, yet moments stood out like sharply focused photographs. The warm torrent of water in the baptismal pool. Father Rob smudging chrism, the anointing oil, on her forehead. Tasting the Body and Blood of Christ for the first time. Hot tears on her face. Father Rob's eyes, with tears, as he gave Jesus to her.

Jessica danced with Harold; they recalled the catechumen who had worn white pants for his baptism. When he had knelt in the baptismal pool and Father Rob had poured water over him, Cody's pants became transparent, and suddenly everyone could see his bright turquoise bikini underpants underneath. Cody could hardly grab a towel fast enough.

Jessica and Harold were still laughing when Father Rob came up beside her and, mock-formally, asked, "May I cut in?"

"Certainly." Harold retreated, grinning.

Jessica turned smiling to face the priest. "It's been a long night. You must be exhausted." She edged from the center of the room as she spoke, away from the dance floor. She didn't want to dance anymore.

"I'm kind of going on fumes." Father Rob's face showed gray smudges under the eyes. "How are you?"

"Fantastic. It's been great. Everything I expected, and more, much more." Jessica picked up her cup of Champagne again and sipped.

"I'm really proud of you, Jess. You've come a long way."

"Baby," Jessica added, pretending to smoke a cigarette.

Father Rob laughed. They stood together for a moment, listening to the music and watching the last few parishioners dancing. Harold was helping Caroline clean up the refreshments, and people were beginning to leave.

"I should go, too," she said.

"Listen, Jessica, I have to tell you something. Can I walk you to your car?"

She nodded, and retrieved her coat and gift bag and flowers from the chair where she'd left them. Father Rob held open the glass door. They walked outside into the chilly night. A sliver of a crescent moon was just cresting the horizon. Their shoes crunched on the gritty pavement. At Jessica's car, she unlocked the door and put her things in the back seat. She turned around to face him, seeing his face shadowed in the glimmer of moon and stars. Dew dampened the air.

"What did you want to tell me?"

"I'm going to announce it tomorrow at all the Masses, but you won't be there, since you came tonight, will you?"

"No, I'm going home for Easter."

"Ah," he said, hesitating. But then, "I'm leaving St. Justin. You know that assignment I told you about, at the chancery office? I'm going to take it."

"Oh, no!" She couldn't help the shock in her voice. "What made you change your mind?"

"The Bishop did. Unfortunately I have no choice in the matter. He calls, I go. That's the way it works." His voice, almost disembodied in the darkness, was resigned.

"It's not fair."

"I made a promise of obedience. I have to be faithful to that."

"When do you leave?"

"In three weeks."

"That's no time at all!"

"I know."

She closed her eyes and shook her head. *You mean so much to me, you saved me, you brought me to life again.* Not one thought she could say out loud. Her eyes pricked with tears again. The unsayable formed a boundary between them. *Don't leave me, not yet.*

He leaned against her car, his arms folded across his chest, his gaze cast down.

"I'm sorry you have to go," Jessica finally said.

"I'm sorry, too. I wanted to tell you tonight; I didn't want you to think that I didn't care how you felt," he said, stumbling over words, unlike she'd ever seen him before.

Was there a subtext in his words? What was the sum of all he had said—did it equal something more? She still couldn't tell. *You're imagining things. Get over it.*

"Thanks," she said simply. "For everything you've done for me. This was the most important night of my life, I think." She shivered in the chill. "The first night of my new life."

"That it was." Father Rob turned to her. "You've done well, Jess. You'll be all right." He heaved a sigh. "And so will I."

"I hope so." She moved to open the car door. Father Rob stood aside and held the door open for her. "Take care."

Because it felt right, it seemed okay, she hugged him, felt him holding her, chest, arms, cheeks pressed together. What was there would never be enough. She saw the priest in her rearview mirror as she drove away, standing alone in the dark empty lot, watching her go.

In three weeks, he would be gone from her life.

Easter

CHAPTER THIRTY-TWO

On the first day of May, Rob loaded books in a box. *The Documents of Vatican II*, all the binders and books on adult catechesis and RCIA, his Latin-English dictionary, his Schillebeeckx, his Rahner, his Dulles, his Küng—all left over from the seminary—and an oversized volume of prints by Corita which wouldn't fit into any box. He left it perched on top of the stack.

The creamy walls of Rob's bedroom and sitting room were bare now, all the photos packed away in bubble wrap. Drawers protruded, emptied of their contents, and three suitcases lay flopped open, revealing dress socks, clerical shirts, boxer shorts in neat piles within.

On Rob's desk, a long list urged him on to the next task. *Say goodbye to RCIA*, check. Like abandoning his own children. He had said, "You'll be fine, you've done the hard part, just keep coming on Tuesdays for another month. The new priest will be here next week, and he'll finish the program with you." Inside, he felt a helpless clawing, the sense of feeble imbalance as if the wind had been knocked out of him. He kept wanting to gasp for breath. Jessica sat through his RCIA announcement, her hands folded neatly in her lap, her eyes wide. She gave him a tight smile but didn't speak as she left last Tuesday.

Then Rob had spoken with all the committees in the parish, and all the ministries; the adult choir (Jessica there again, meeting his eyes), the Knights of Columbus, and the First Communion class at the school; the gardener, the housekeeper, and Luis, the seminarian from St. Joseph's;

then the babysitting co-op volunteers (and again she was there). So many goodbyes.

A priest from the diocese came to take over Masses while Rob packed, until the new priest arrived. Rob cocooned himself in the rectory, away from the familiar faces of St. Justin Martyr, stowed his possessions into boxes and carried them out to his Jeep.

He scanned his list to see what he'd yet to do.

"Need any help?"

Rob turned at Jessica's voice. "Hi. What are you doing here?"

"The door was open. I just came by to say goodbye. Again, I mean. And to offer some assistance if you need any." Her hair was captured in an elastic band, wayward strands working themselves out in spite of it. Jessica was dressed, like Rob, in jeans and a man's work shirt with the sleeves rolled up.

"Well, if you're desperate to help, you can grab a box and help me load. But I'm almost done. Then I'm out of here." Rob jerked his thumb in the direction of Joan of Arc parish, smiling wryly as he took up a box.

Jessica picked up a carton of books and followed him out to his vehicle. The car was fully loaded after a half dozen trips, the room almost empty but for furniture that belonged to the rectory. His vacant desk. His bed, stripped bare, sheets piled in a basket for the housekeeper. Nothing left behind.

They stood at the car, dusting off their hands on their jeans, talking about the Vigil and RCIA. Rob listened to her voice, silently pleased at the changes in her over the past few months: more confident, unburdened, she was charming and funny, with a flip way of answering, and she had lost the hunted rabbit posture.

"What are you looking at?" She twisted a finger in a loose curl.

His eyes followed the twirl of her finger into the hair, rich chestnut with gold-red lights in the late spring sunshine. He wanted to bury his hands in the mass of curls. He indulged himself the moment of reverie. *It doesn't matter, I'm leaving here, never see her again.* "Nothing."

They stood by the Jeep in the warmth of the sun. Rob could see the rectory garden, all gold and pink in the sunshine, roses thick with blooms, daisies and geraniums shouldered up to the rectory, jasmine cascading on a trellis, their scents sweetening the air. "I have to go," Rob finally said. "Got to turn in my keys, get going." *Here's looking at you, kid.*

"Yeah, me, too. I'll see you, I guess, maybe sometime at the cathedral or something." Her voice ended on an upnote, a question, a suggestion of a plan, perhaps.

"Listen, let's keep in touch; give me a call sometime if you're in the neighborhood." He knew she wouldn't, but he needed to say it, to give himself something to look forward to. "We can have a cup of coffee or something."

"Sure. That sounds nice. St. Joan of Arc. Got it." She smiled a wan smile at him, as if she were about to cry. But her eyes were dry. "Take care of yourself. And thanks for everything."

They hugged goodbye, his face pressed to hers, his hand for an instant in the tangle of her hair, kissing the pale cheek as she kissed his rough shadow.

Rob found his room at St. Joan of Arc rectory by its smell of old carpet and mothballs and not enough fresh air; the austere walls of his quarters were white and stark, the bed firm, the furniture relics from the days of sunken living rooms and lava lamps. Rob dragged the metal desk toward the window and pushed two tan vinyl-covered chairs together to create a sitting area. He tripped repeatedly over the brown shag carpet as he moved about the room. The textured glass of the windows annoyed him; a branch outside his window was a green blur, and that was all he could see. Below, the parochial schoolyard backed up to the rectory; cries of playing children and the yard supervisor's whistle filtered into his room, a sort of white noise. Older boys played basketball at recess and lunch, the dusty orange ball whumping with frequency against the siding of the rectory. Rob earned a headache by afternoon.

At dinner he went down and met the cook, Evelina, and broke bread with Father Peter Callahan, the Irish-born old pastor of St. Joan. Dinner was some kind of overcooked casserole with rice and too much paprika; Rob's stomach groaned sourly for the rest of the evening. His bedsprings squeaked. The blankets smelled different, the sheets scented with some other detergent, and the new synthetic foam pillow flattened overnight, with a permanent dent from his head.

Rob lay with his head in the shallow cleft and looked at the ceiling. He saw the tiny cracks that tessellated the ceiling toward the corner where, inevitably, a spider crouched, and watched how the light of dawn strained across his room through bubbled windows. It wasn't much of a start.

CHAPTER THIRTY-THREE

Canon 1055: 1. The matrimonial covenant is by its nature ordered toward the good of the spouses and the procreation of offspring.

Rob read the commentary on Canon 1055 from the dense *Code of Canon Law* that rested on his battered desk, with 1,200 tissue-thin pages. He sat in his new office at the Chancery, with its squeaky chair and contrary filing cabinets, and studied the section regarding marriage. Rob tried to stay out of everyone else's way; he felt like a seminarian again, bumbling and incompetent. He knew little of the nuances of canon law, other than what he'd learned in one semester at the seminary. Rob wasn't much use to anyone in the office, not to the secretaries who bustled around, referring to annulment cases in an offhand manner, joking in Latin; he was of no use at all to the three canon lawyers, priests who sat in their own offices reading current cases and arguing to each other across the hallway.

"Hey, Ted, what are you doing with the Schmidt case?"

"It's a formal case."

"Yeah, but he's baptized and she isn't. That's a Favor of the Faith. Pauline Privilege. Canon 1143. Look it up."

"Yeah, but it's easier to make it a formal case than to send it to Rome. 'Intention against permanence on the part of the Petitioner.' Case closed."

Rob listened to shop talk and banter and tried to take an interest. What he wanted to know was who were the Schmidts, Mr. and Mrs.? Were they a middle-aged couple who had split after many years of infidelities? Were they young marrieds, together just a few months, too immature to make the commitment? What faces matched those names? Whose heart hurt, whose children cried, whose lives were split apart with the proper phrase in Latin?

> *Canon 1058: All persons who are not prohibited by law can contract marriage.*

Despite his years as a pastor, Rob had little experience contending with annulments and dispensations. Annulment was a process required by the Church to clear a former marriage from the books, which then allowed a Catholic to remarry, or permitted one's current marriage to become a sacrament. Dispensations, which were exceptions to the canon law, could be granted to Catholics who wished, for example, to marry non-Catholics or cousins, or who were underage. At St. Justin Martyr, whenever Rob's parishioners needed annulments or some such, he used to forward the details to the Chancery Office and let the canon lawyers clean up the mess. Now here he was, broom and dustpan in hand, trying to learn how to sweep.

> *Canon 1060: Marriage enjoys the favor of the law; consequently, when a doubt exists, the validity of a marriage is to be upheld until the contrary is proven.*

There were just four ways a marriage could be declared invalid and made null. Flipping through the massive *Code*, Rob would have sworn that there must be hundreds of types, but no, one of the canon lawyers assured him, just four; the marriage canons in the *Code* were myriad permutations of those simple four.

Rob worked through the pages with the diligence he'd once applied to calculus and chemistry. Lack of form, Favor of the Faith, Pauline Privilege or Petrine Privilege.

The hours ticked by; the staff went to lunch, came back, went home. Rob, reading page after page of canon law commentaries, rubbed his eyes from time to time and considered getting an eye exam. He made notes on index cards which he marked according to a system with yellow and pink highlighter pens: specific canon laws, what-if scenarios, typical cases. At four o'clock, the office closed. Rob took his cards and the voluminous *Code* and went home to St. Joan of Arc.

At the rectory, Rob ate the early supper Evelina cooked for him and Father Callahan, a brown stew with very soft vegetables and meat so well boiled that he barely had to chew it. After Evelina went home and Father Callahan retired—at seven o'clock, for God's sake, it was still light out—Rob poured the cook's weak coffee down the sink and made his own brew, strong and flavorful.

He took his mug upstairs to his room, depressed by the brownness of the place: brown carpet, brown paneling, brown food. Even the towels were brown. There was no one to call; at least, Rob didn't want to call anyone, despite his desperation for company. With a sigh, Rob settled himself in the vinyl recliner that didn't recline and flicked on the TV. The same tired reruns were on, or new shows so inane Rob couldn't stomach them. He finally settled on an endless documentary about the Kennedy assassination in grainy footage, explosions of a man's skull, conspiracy theories, until he fell asleep in the chair.

He dreamed of milky flesh, caressing fingers, the electric tingle of skin against skin.

> *Canon 1061: A valid marriage between baptized persons is called ratified only if it has not been consummated; it is called ratified and consummated if the parties have performed between themselves in a human manner the conjugal act which is per se suitable for the generation of children, to which marriage is ordered by its very nature and by which the spouses become one flesh.*

In the morning Rob arose and said the early Mass for Father Callahan, who had an appointment with his podiatrist. Rob had asked to be put on the regular schedule for daily Mass, but the old priest didn't want to trouble Rob.

"You're busy at the Chancery. You don't need this extra work."

"But I want to. I miss saying Mass."

The old priest considered. "Why don't you take one of the masses on Sunday, and leave the dailies to me. If I have to go out, you can cover for me."

Rob wasn't satisfied with the arrangements, but he was only a guest there, in residence, and didn't want to argue with his host. *I'm not pastor anymore. I'm a guest, that's all.*

> *Canon 1075: 1. The supreme authority of the Church alone has the competence to declare when divine law prohibits or voids a marriage.*

Rob had married more than a hundred couples since his ordination. Each couple spent several weeks in marriage preparation courses, the Pre-Cana or Engaged Encounter. He would meet with the couple and provide a compatibility test, and talk to them about expectations and the realities of married life; after the six weeks, Rob felt that he knew something about the couple and their chances for success.

At the Chancery Office, the marriages were unmade, stamped, filed away, the annulment certificate sent, and the case closed. True, the marriages were probably crumbled beyond redemption by then, and only devoted Catholics even sought annulments anymore. Rob wasn't naive, thinking that with a little love and faith, the problems would be solved. He knew from his parishioners that some marriages became a living hell. St. Justin's Divorced Catholics group had introduced him to some of the most wounded people he'd ever known.

Rob tried to think of *Schmidt v. Schmidt (nee Terrence)*, faceless names he knew nothing about, as just another case. But when marriage was such a precious gift, a mirage beyond his earthly reach, he hated to think of one dying. How could they end it, Mr. and Mrs. Schmidt, just walk away? How could they let each other go?

> *Canon 1087: Persons who are in holy orders invalidly attempt marriage.*

There it was. The zinger. *Not that I've attempted it.* In black letters, it stated the rule with no ifs, ands, or buts. Rob wrote it on an index card and added it to his stack.

Early in his priestly career, he had traveled on a tour to Rome with some parishioners from the diocese. One of the highlights of the tour was visiting the Catacombs beneath the cobbled streets of the ancient city. Below, where the dead were buried, the earliest Christians celebrated the Last Supper, as Jesus had taught them. Down in the darkness, surrounded by old bones, in fear for their lives, the Christians affirmed their faith in the everlasting life in Christ.

Here, in the jumbled Chancery Office, Rob was encircled by overstuffed filing cabinets crammed with the relics of dead marriages. He simply couldn't find a way to celebrate that.

CHAPTER THIRTY-FOUR

"Good evening, Father Pastor." Lawrence handed Cesar a chilled bottle of Champagne as he walked into the rectory of St. Cecile.

Cesar grinned, his round face dimpled. "Nothing is certain yet." Monsignor Grimmley had suffered a stroke just after Easter and had since removed to a convalescent home; Cesar would run the parish until a permanent decision came from the personnel board, but everyone expected Cesar to be appointed the next pastor.

"Shame on you two, celebrating the decline of an old man! And a monsignor, at that!" William sat, reclined on the sofa, his long legs crossed at the knee, hands clasped behind his head. "Where's your Christian charity?"

"It's been sucked out of me," Lawrence said.

"I'll bet."

Lawrence made a face at William as he sat down. "Congratulations anyway, Cesar. You're almost a pastor."

Cesar smiled self-consciously as he struggled to open the bottle.

"Oh, let me do that, dear." William rose to open the Champagne. He peeled the foil and untwisted the wire cage, then gently worked the cork out with his thumbs. It leaped out with a joyous pop, and William poured the bubbling pale liquid into wine glasses.

"Cesar, you must get better barware than this, now that you control the checkbook. It's vulgar to drink Champagne out of Wal-Mart wine glasses. Get some Waterford, for God's sake." William distributed the glasses. The three priests clinked them together. "Hail, Caesar."

"Hail, Caesar," Lawrence echoed. They sipped their Champagne.

"And how about you, Mozart?" William asked. "What's with the music these days?"

Lawrence grimaced. "Still plugging away. I have a few bits and pieces to finish, and then I still have to clean up the score and record a demo. It's due in two weeks. I shouldn't even be out tonight." He heard the soaring notes of the *Amen* in his head. *Please God, let it all work.*

"Well, then, here's to the music!" William raised his glass.

"To the music!"

Lawrence waved a hand to stop them. "Don't—you'll curse my luck!"

"Well, then, what else can we toast?" William poured more Champagne. A look crossed his face, and he smiled. "I know. To Father Rob, canon lawyer."

Lawrence set down his glass. "Has anyone heard from him since he moved?"

Cesar shook his head. "I saw him right before Easter. I have not even been to the Chancery since the Vigil. It has been too busy here." He sat in an armchair. "I wish I knew the story."

"And you don't know anything?" William looked at Lawrence.

Lawrence didn't want to explain what had really happened. It was too mixed up, would look wrong. As if he was jealous, or worse. Lawrence shrugged. "We're not exactly talking. He's still mad at us, you know. From dinner that night," he added.

"Touchy, touchy."

"All I know is that the Bishop gave him the Chancery job and he moved to Joan of Arc. So Rob's with Callahan in that old barn of a rectory."

"That must be fun. Shall we pay him a visit?" William wriggled his eyebrows wickedly.

"Oh, I don't think so," Lawrence cautioned. "I don't think he wants to hear from us right now." Lawrence swallowed the last of his Champagne. *At least he's away from her.* That gave Lawrence some comfort. But was it worth the price to save him from temptation? Lawrence had risked their friendship on a woman, and Rob wasn't even speaking to him anymore. Lawrence wouldn't be able to save him if there was a next time.

"I agree with Lawrence," Cesar added. "He was very unhappy when last I saw him."

"Spoilsports."

"But guess who has taken Rob's place at St. Justin?" Cesar said, his face lighting with a certain glee.

"Sleazer, how do you know these delicious tidbits?" William marveled.

"I just hear things, that is all." He shrugged modestly.

"Well, do tell, dear. Who?" William cupped his ear.

"Brandon McDonald."

"Oooh, nooo!" William crowed.

"I thought he was gone. I thought he went to Gemma Springs and never came back."

"No, he is back, and he is sober. He *says* he is sober." Cesar raised his brows. "Maybe he is, God be willing."

"Even when he's sober, he's not going to win any prizes. He's so straight." Lawrence corrected himself. "I mean, conservative."

"Poor St. Justin. That's a far cry from warm, fuzzy, lovable Father Rob." William sighed tragically.

"Hey, have either of you read that nun's book, the ordination one?" Lawrence asked, switching gears as smoothly as possible.

"No," Cesar said. "It is against my religion."

William burst out laughing. "That was very good, Cesar. You've just earned your merit badge in humor." He laughed some more and sipped his Champagne. "As a matter of fact, I have read the book. Sister Patrice makes these outrageous claims about the ordination of women and so on, and I sit there and laugh, and the next thing, I find myself saying, well, why not? Then I remember, I'm Catholic. That's why not." He laughed again. "How about you, Lawrence? Have you read it?"

"No thanks. I live with that all the time. Patrice DuLac must be Therese's twin sister. Separated at birth."

"You both forget that I actually know Patrice," Cesar said. "I went on her retreat at Hagia Sophia, before she got ejected. She is really a very nice woman."

"That's her problem. She's a woman. She should have been born a man," William said.

"Unlike you, right?"

"Very funny." William sniffed and tossed his head. "What I find *tres* amusing is that letter from the Bishop we're supposed to read on Sunday. 'Don't read that book!' It's all so Catholic League. Try telling parishioners they can't do something, and they'll be pounding at the gates wanting to do it."

"Like I have time to deal with that letter," Lawrence added. "And I can hear it now—people crying, 'Oh, censorship, First Amendment, you priests can't tell me what to do, boo hoo hoo!' I'm just going to leave it to Tom. He's the almighty pastor, not me."

"If Bishop says to read the letter, then we read it," Cesar said firmly. "The Conference of Bishops does not want people to read Sister Patrice's book. Bishop does not want people to read her book. So we read his letter and stand behind it."

Lawrence was taken aback by Cesar's new sense of authority. "Attaboy, Sleazer." But he didn't want to talk Church anymore. His stomach rumbled. "When's dinner? I'm famished."

CHAPTER THIRTY-FIVE

Rob took Saturdays off now instead of Fridays, but he spent them at loose ends. No one called except his mother, twice a week, like clockwork. Cesar had left his position at the diocese to run St. Cecile; Rob no longer saw him in the Chancery's halls, a mixed blessing, because while Rob was still angry at Cesar and the others, he was lonely, too. Lawrence had stopped calling at Easter, and Rob couldn't call back, not yet, maybe not ever. The silence between them weighed upon him. Their separation left a void in his life like a death; Rob couldn't keep it off his mind. Lawrence lurked there like a shadow of what used to be.

And beyond that, like a shadow of that shadow, lay the echo of Jessica's last words to him, the ring of her laughter, the curl of her hair around his fingers as they hugged goodbye. He couldn't call her, either, and wouldn't. St. Justin Martyr floated away behind him like a leaf on a stream, and there was nothing but to stop moping and go on.

But the parish of St. Joan of Arc could never supplant his old parish. At St. Justin, Rob would have roamed the rectory, walked the grounds, or strolled around the school. Almost any weekend, some event was in progress at that vibrant parish: CYO basketball games, fund-raisers, retreats for the various groups. At St. Justin, Rob might have joined in some activity, or perhaps gone to spend the day with parishioners at their homes. Even if he just stayed around the parish, he would have made his coffee and lain on the sofa with a newspaper, in peace and comfort. Despite the loneliness Rob had felt there, it still felt something like home to him. But he couldn't get used to Joan of Arc.

Few parishioners at St. Joan bothered to meet him, a mere priest-in-residence. One lace-curtain Irish woman introduced herself as Mrs. Quinn and then spent the next ten minutes bragging about her son, a seminarian. "My son is helping out at the Church of the Resurrection with lovely Father Lawrence," she said, somewhere in the middle of her boast. Rob tried to avoid the woman, but then he discovered she was the church secretary. Every morning as he left for the Chancery office, Mrs. Quinn called a lilting greeting to him from the office by the front door; her presence was a reminder of Lawrence that he couldn't evade.

On this Saturday, Rob waited until the kitchen was clear, then poured Evalina's weak coffee down the drain and made a fresh strong batch. Rob walked to the sitting room and tried to relax on the couch, but there was something awkward about the action. He couldn't get comfortable. He was a stranger there, only a guest. He could hardly put his feet up, even if no one was there to see. He sat up stiffly and drank his coffee.

The large empty house creaked. Father Callahan had gone off to the hospital to visit a parishioner who lay in traction. Evalina had the day off. Mrs. Quinn didn't come on weekends. Rob waited for the day to wane in slow, miserable minutes. The sound of voices, of car doors slamming in the driveway roused him from his funk. Rob leaned toward the window to see who had arrived, then jumped to answer the door.

Patrick greeted Rob with a bear hug. Kate stood by, her wriggling son in her arms. She smiled at Rob as he kissed her cheek.

Rob was glad no one was around; he could play the host in the strange rectory without interruptions. Patrick and Kate came into the sitting room. Their faces reflected peace and contentment. Rob couldn't take his eyes off the couple. Kate looked lovely, all shining gold hair and indulgent smiles as she played with her son. Patrick gazed on them. They formed a triptych of love, a holy family.

"How are you?" Rob asked, though he could tell: All was very well indeed.

Kate didn't answer, instead ran her left hand through her hair, slowly, the light glinting off her gold ring. Patrick turned to Rob. "Can you guess?" He paused a few seconds for effect. "We're married." Kate wagged her ringed finger at Rob.

"Congratulations!" Rob shook Patrick's hand. "I should have guessed. When?"

"About a month ago."

"Thirty-two days," corrected Kate.

"That didn't take long," Rob said.

"We were ready. It's not like we had to go through Engaged Encounter or anything." Patrick eyed Rob with his clear gray eyes. "So, now you're my only friend, huh?"

"Am I?"

"Well, no one else is talking to me. I've hopped the fence. I'm a traitor. What do you think?"

"I know the feeling," Rob said. "But no one knew where you were, for one thing. You were incommunicado. Where are you living now?"

"Oh, we got an apartment in the City. I'm teaching at a private high school—history and PE, can you believe it?"

"I can't believe anyone would hire you."

"And I can't believe how hard people have to work out there." Patrick raised his hands. "These hands were made for chalices, not for calluses."

Rob laughed at the old joke. "That's how the other half lives."

Kate shushed them. "He's almost asleep!"

They watched Kate rock the baby in her arms, slowly moving around the room, rocking and humming tunelessly, softly, until the child's eyes closed in sleep. Patrick got a blanket from the diaper bag, laid it on the carpet, and watched as Kate gingerly laid the sleeping boy on his back. The baby's mouth, a pink bow, made sucking motions. His arms curled inward, tiny fingers gripped in fists, then he relaxed and his arms went limp. His thick lashes lay dark against his pale cheeks.

Kate moved to the sofa and flopped back. "Ahh, my arms were going numb!"

Patrick sat next to her and put his arm around her shoulders. "It's so good to be able to do this, to touch her, to just put my arm around her and not have to hide anymore," Patrick remarked to Rob.

"Tell me about Gemma Springs. What happened, anyway?" Rob sat in the chair near the window.

"Well, let's see," Patrick laid a finger against his cheek as if pondering. "First some of my dear friends told tales about me, then I was jerked away and sent off to the loony bin with a busload of pedophiles, some alcoholics, an overeater, and two other guys like me who happened to have girlfriends. We had to sit in a circle and talk about our feelings every day. I couldn't call anyone; I couldn't go anywhere. I just sat there, trying to pray and figure out what I wanted to do." Patrick took Kate's hand from her lap and held it like a treasure. "At least it was beautiful there. I stayed in a little cabin, a gorgeous little adobe place looking up at those salmon-pink mountains. Except that I was essentially in jail." He half-laughed. "The Bishop sent me there to get over Kate, but all it did was make me surer than ever. Can you imagine, they were willing to pay child support, but they didn't want me to ever see my son again?"

"Well, what did you expect?"

"Hey, we were following the letter of the law; we never used birth control, not once, did we, Kate?" He winked at her.

"Patrick!" She shushed them again.

"Well, you have to admit, having the baby complicated things," Rob said, more quietly.

"Well, yes and no," Patrick admitted. "To be brutally honest, it wasn't really a mistake. I mean, of course the pregnancy was bound to happen. We both knew it. It was just a matter of time. And I must have wanted it to happen, somehow, subconsciously, or it never would have gone that far." He chuckled. "So much for celibacy. I guess I just wasn't cut out to be a priest."

Patrick's nonchalance needled Rob. "Pardon my saying so, but shouldn't you have thought of all this before you were ordained?"

Patrick wasn't offended. He ran a hand through his hair and smiled his lazy smile. "Well, I guess so, but my parents always pushed me to be a priest; they've been talking about my vocation since I was about three years old. I always felt destined for the priesthood. And then there I was in the seminary, and then ordained. I just went with the flow."

Rob nodded, understanding.

"It was good being a priest. I liked it. But it just didn't work for me; there are other things in life that I want." Patrick's arm tightened around Kate's shoulder, and Rob watched how she nestled into the embrace.

"I used to say something to the married couples who came to me for counseling," Patrick went on. "If one of them was cheating and the other one didn't know why, I would say, 'a person doesn't go looking unless there's something missing at home. What's missing?' So I asked myself, and it was obvious. I wanted a wife. I couldn't stand celibacy. The 'marriage' went sour, so to speak. So I went looking." Patrick shrugged off the magnitude of his actions. "But I only left the priesthood, not the Church."

"Well, now you *are* out of the Church," Rob reminded them. "You're both cradle Catholics. Doesn't it bother you to be excommunicated?"

"Not at the moment," said Patrick, glancing at Kate. She shook her head. "All it takes is a little paperwork. I'll apply for a laicization, and then I'll be just a regular guy again. It may take a while, but eventually we'll be back in. I'm not too worried about it."

"Really?"

"Really." Patrick assured him. "Why are you so obsessed about this? Are you thinking of leaving, too?"

"No," Rob said, little louder than he intended. He covered his mouth, glancing at the baby. "I'm just wondering," he whispered. "I would just want to be really sure of what I was doing, of how permanent an exile it might be." He turned to Kate. "Don't misunderstand me, Kate. I don't disapprove. I'm just trying to get some answers."

"Rob, Patrick's fine. He's much happier since he left and there's no more sneaking around. He's so good with Matthew, and it's just wonderful being a family." She caressed Patrick's knee next to her.

"She's right," Patrick added. "For the first time in my life, I'm perfectly content. I've got a half-way decent job, a beautiful wife, a sweet little son. The only thing that's not okay right now is my parents. My dad's in rigor mortis and my mother's having fainting spells or something. But it's not their life. It's mine. They'll come around, eventually."

Rob considered his own mother and almost shuddered. News of him leaving the priesthood would put her in the grave. He pushed the thought aside and asked his guests, "How about some coffee?"

Later, as his friends left, Rob gripped Patrick's hand and said, "Let me know if you need anything. If I can help out."

"Thanks, Rob." Patrick walked down the steps, and then turned back. "And if you need anything, maybe an impartial ear, someone outside all of this—" he gestured at the rectory, "—just give me a call. We'll talk."

CHAPTER THIRTY-SIX

The choir began the entrance antiphon. From her position on the choir's risers, second row, soprano side, Jessica could see the new priest center in the procession. She hadn't realized that a priest could own his own vestments until she saw the chasuble. Jessica had thought of the vestments as part of the church's furnishings. Rob's chasuble for Easter had been a heavy brocade, white on white. This one was white with gold stitching and an embroidered gold cross on the front and back. She marked the variance as another difference, another departure from how things used to be at St. Justin Martyr. The way things were *not* anymore.

Gold and white banners still swagged the church, and the Easter lilies that remained in good health clustered before the altar. Jessica spied some RCIA friends and smiled hello to them from the risers. The choir rose and sang again, then remained standing for the Gospel reading.

> *For I was hungry and you gave me food, I was thirsty and you gave me drink, a stranger and you welcomed me, naked and you clothed me, ill and you cared for me, in prison and you visited me.*

The words stayed in her head as they sat for the homily. The new priest's voice was soft and whispery, as if the man couldn't catch his breath, and his voice fell and rose, so that sometimes his words were indistinct.

"I'm Father Brandon McDonald. I'm your new pastor here at St. Justin

Martyr, replacing Father Souza, who, as you know, has moved on to a position in the diocese." He said something else indistinguishable. "…don't want there to be any rumors going around, so I'm going to tell you now. I'm a recovering alcoholic."

The parishioners didn't gasp, but from her seat in the choir, Jessica saw eyes widen and eyebrows shoot upwards.

"There will be some changes around here," he began, launching into a list of his plans for the future of St. Justin. "We'll have First Friday services and Benediction on a regular monthly basis. And I'll reinstate the Legion of Mary as well."

Jessica had no idea what Father McDonald was talking about. Later she asked the soprano next to her.

"Conservative stuff. Legion of Mary—good Lord, that's so old-fashioned! We stopped doing that when Monsignor Finley died." The woman made a face. "There goes the parish."

Jessica listened to the creaky-whispery voice of the priest. When the choir filed up for Communion, she got a closer look at him. His hair was thick as thatch, salt and pepper, wiry, cut close like a lawn, and apparently didn't respond well to brushing. His eyes seemed bulbous, loose in their sockets; tiny rivers ranged red across the whites and disappeared into the iris.

"Body of Christ," he said, not even looking at her, not even seeing her, a person who came humbly to receive the Body of Christ, the sacrament of Holy Communion. He pushed the Host into her hand. She stepped away, pausing to consume the Host before the altar, blessed herself and turned to receive the Cup. But there was no cup offered—a concession, apparently, to the man's addiction. Jessica felt the sticky starch of the wafer cling to her throat. She returned to her seat in the choir, clearing her throat. She prayed briefly, and then prepared to sing the meditation song.

The choir director gestured and the choir members rose, flipping their binders open to the proper song.

> When I was weak you strengthened me.
> When I was outcast, you brought me in.
> When I was frightened, you comforted me.

Everything about St. Justin reminded her of Father Rob. Even the song, which he had suggested for his last Sunday. They had, with tears, sung him farewell.

Now nothing was left here of him but a memory. Not his voice. Not his eyes. Not the man.

CHAPTER THIRTY-SEVEN

The last note echoed in the music room. It was done.

Lawrence clicked the recorder off, then put his head in his arms, leaned over the black and white keyboard and squeezed his eyes shut. Tears blurred his vision, his close-up view of his pressed shirt-sleeve, the golden down on his arm, the shadowed keyboard beneath him. Lawrence sniffled and wiped his cheeks with his fingertips. It was really done. His Mass was written and recorded, as perfect as it could be. And he had made the June deadline, by eleven days yet.

A week of solitude after Easter had blessed him with the focus he needed. Father Tom left on his post-Easter vacation for a week in Cancun. Therese also vanished, gone off to commune with squirrels or to a seminar in Taiko drumming, something quirky enough to captivate Tom and really annoy Lawrence. Lawrence sent Sean the seminarian home, and called in weekend-supply priests from the seminary to cover the Mass schedule while he worked. It was, after all, Lawrence's vacation, too, even if he stayed holed in his own room.

An empty rectory was bliss. Lawrence walked about in his bathrobe or faded sweats, sometimes nude, ate all the Italian food he liked—with butter, real butter, not the vegan-soy-margarine that Therese kept in the fridge—and worked till all hours of the night. One morning Lawrence had awakened at the piano, his hands still on the keys, his forehead imprinted from the scrolled music rack before him. Charming, he thought, rubbing his stiff neck. But it didn't matter. The music flowed from him, embellishment, austerity, a delicate tissue of scrim between the two that kept the balance between medieval and modern.

Completed pages filled a binder at his side, thickening over the days like a waxing moon. He turned his face to the ceiling, eyes shut, and spanned the octaves with spread fingers. In blindness, he more than played, he sensed the notes, felt their resonance in his bones, in his teeth, drank them like well-aged wine, and carried their shadows with him like a palimpsest into memory.

Tom returned, bronzed and cheerful, and went about his work, leaving Lawrence alone. Lawrence was on a roll, trying to beat the deadline, trying to finish before Therese came back to haunt him. Then Therese called and said she was extending her leave; even so, Lawrence was still anxious and, pressed for time, continued his assault on the music. He wrote the score by hand with his Italian fountain pen, transcribed it on his computer, and then recorded it in his own little studio.

At last he finished.

Lawrence addressed the heavy envelope with a sense of disbelief. The disk slid into its cardboard cover. The white sheets with their black notations slipped into the envelope with ease. He licked the flap and pressed it tight, then placed the envelope by the door to take downtown and mail the next morning. He felt the disquieting sensation of suddenly having nothing to do. His fingers twitched in his pockets. The music still careened through his head, joyful, persistent.

Any other time he would have called Rob and gone out to celebrate as they had in August, when Lawrence had the first news of his project. And he wanted to call Rob; he really did. But he couldn't. Not now. The chill between the two priests had hardened into frost. Lawrence waited to hear what happened to Rob through the grapevine, over drinks, at diocesan meetings. Would Rob leave the Church for that woman? Or would he, could he still get over her? At every church function that Lawrence attended, the priests gossiped about Rob, and they would ask Lawrence what Rob thought or what he was planning. Lawrence smiled enigmatically, shrugged slightly as if he couldn't say. But the truth was that he didn't even know.

Lawrence neither admitted nor denied his role in Rob's marching orders. *I did what I had to do.* She had come between them. He had never met her, whatever her name was, though he recalled seeing her from a distance at the Rite of Election—a redhead, of all things; who could ask for a more perfect Scarlet Woman? All curves and big green eyes, some sob story at the ready. Lawrence could almost sniff out the attraction between them; it hung in the air like the keen scent of sex. *Somebody had to save him.* So Lawrence martyred himself to save the man, sacrificed their friendship for his beloved. Few could love a friend so much. *I call you friends...love one another,* said the Gospel. But Lawrence couldn't talk about it to the others; he just didn't feel up to the banter of the boys in black.

And there was no one to share his news with now.

Lawrence took a shower and drove into the City, to the club he liked to visit. At least there he didn't have to explain, to justify, or to put up with the politics. A stunningly handsome man leaned against the bar as Lawrence walked in. *No bullshit*, read his tight T-shirt, rippling over a tan muscular body. Their eyes met. The message flashed.

Perfect, Lawrence thought. *No bullshit.*

Pentecost

CHAPTER THIRTY-EIGHT

On the Friday before Pentecost, Rob finished work at the Chancery at four thirty. But instead of returning to St. Joan of Arc, he drove back to his childhood parish, to St. Peter, in the run-down working class district where he'd grown up. He disliked seeing the wreck of what used to be a humble, tidy neighborhood. Now the old Queen Anne and Victorian-style houses had degenerated into semi-slums. Cars parked haphazardly on the remains of lawns, broken appliances littered empty lots, and Rob saw what looked like brazen drug deals on several familiar corners as he drove toward the church.

Rob remembered how vibrant the neighborhood had been when he was a child: the old Portuguese men visiting on street corners, Mexican housewives pulling their carts home from the grocery store, and kids on bikes, on sidewalks, everywhere. Rob spent his waking hours riding his bike around the blocks, or playing football or baseball in the wide streets all afternoon, while the sun cast its last golden rays on shining windows. When he was late, his mother called him from the porch, and if he caused trouble, neighbors would scold him in three different languages.

When Rob went away to the seminary, he felt he had set sail to another world, a glorious realm where the words were richer, had more meaning and depth somehow. There was something elevated in the faith he found there, in the purity of a syllogism, in the clarity of logic. Rob embraced the Catholicism of the learned man, an exalted, prismatic understanding of the Word of God. And when he went home again, and found his mother still clinging to her peasant piety, her house crammed with statues and the brittle collection of Passion Sunday palms, her rosary ever wound around her fingers and a muttered prayer on her lips, he felt as if he had returned to life among the savages.

Rob dared to say as much to Father Anselm on one of his visits home from St. Joseph's. Instead of answering, Father Anselm's hand snaked out and grabbed the short hair at Rob's temple.

"That hurts!"

"Don't let those Sulpicians fill your head with all that high talk," the priest rebuked him.

Rob didn't move or speak for the pain. He eyed Father Anselm, awed by the priest's anger.

"Your mother—the way she prays, the way she believes—that's faith there. Don't sneer at it. It has value. Remember, 'Even the least of these are Mine,'" he gave Rob's hair another tug, then let go. "Don't forget that when you become a priest."

"I won't, Father," Rob had said, rubbing his temple. "I'm sorry."

Rob knocked at the rectory door. No response. He crossed the driveway to the side entrance to the church, pulled the heavy door open, and went in. St. Peter had been remodeled and newly painted since he said his First Mass here years before, its Pre-Vatican II gloom brightened with new windows, lighter colors, and the cheerful splash of a baptismal pool near the foyer.

Rob wandered around, running a hand along the smooth wood of the front pew, admiring the new interior. He paused to glance into the octagonal confessionals but they were vacant, then he passed the chapel, thinking it was empty. Rob stopped when he saw who knelt there, his old pastor, Father Anselm, still in residence though he'd retired two years ago.

"Hello, Father." He spoke quietly, not to startle the elderly priest.

Father Anselm looked up. A smile lit his face. "Hello there, Robert. Good God, boy, it's been a while. I never see you around. I don't get out much, but you'd think I'd spot you once in a while."

"I'm at the diocese now, in the Chancery Office."

"Yes, I heard that from your mother. She calls it the 'chancy office'" Fr. Anselm laughed gently. "Poor woman." He looked up at Rob. "I guess I should say 'poor man.' You come home to talk to me?"

Rob nodded.

"Here, help me up, son." Rob supported Father Anselm's elbow as he got stiffly to his feet. "That's better. Thank you." The old priest brushed the creases from his black trousers. "What's on your mind?"

"Can we talk confidentially?" Rob asked. "It's not a confession—well, it is, of a sort, but not really. More of a head-clearing session. Do you mind?"

"Let's go into the confessional, the big one there, just for privacy, all right?" Father Anselm walked slowly with Rob to the larger of the two confessionals and pulled the door shut behind them. "Have a seat." Father Anselm lowered himself to the other chair. He raised his brows at Rob. "Well?"

Rob took a deep breath. "I hardly know how to start." Father Anselm had heard Rob's first confession as a little boy. But there were words and thoughts and confusion so tangled inside him; he was afraid, because saying them aloud would make them real.

"There's someone in my life," Rob said, but already he'd made a bad start. He backpedaled. "Not even in my life. In my heart." He had to stop, his throat closing in as if he would choke or start to cry. Rob cleared his throat and pressed on.

"We're not involved, not in any tangible way. But I've had this incredible feeling for her, from literally the first time I saw her, if you can believe that. I've counseled her, heard her confession, given her First Communion. I've watched her blossom like a flower."

"She is of age, I hope," Father Anselm said, alarmed. "Robert, you're not saying what I think you're saying, please God."

"Oh, God, no!" Rob burst out laughing. "I mean, yes, she's of age. She's 26. She was in my RCIA group this year. I don't know how it happened—I've been fighting this from the get-go. I push the thoughts away, the daydreams, just shut them out, because it's torture, you know; it's unwise and it's impossible. I've fought it from the beginning. But here I am, snared in my own web."

"Does she share your feelings?" His blue eyes had changed, Rob noticed, paled as if thickened with age. But their gaze was as intent as ever.

"I think so. We've never talked about it; we sort of implied it one time, sort of almost said something about this *feeling*, and then we didn't say it, and the moment passed, and it was better not to because it's out of the question. It's not like she's stalking me." The thought was ludicrous to him.

And yet Jessica had been there, nearby, so many times during the last few months at St. Justin, as if since her confession she needed to stay close, or lose that bond between them; he had grown to expect her presence, and missed her when she was gone.

"We've never done anything sexual, nothing physical, no more than a friendly hug, the same as I gave any other parishioner, and we kissed on the cheek a couple of times." Rob remembered the past several months, reviewed each instance like an open file. "But I knew I wouldn't do more, and the kisses were acceptable in the context of the situation, and I feel confident that it was okay. I'm absolutely sure about that."

"Come on, you sound like a lawyer presenting a case," Father Anselm said. "Is that what they're teaching you over at the Chancery? What I want to know is, do you care for her because of who she is, or, if I may ask, do you just want what you can't have?"

Rob was used to Father Anselm's candor, but the question threw him. He weighed his answer carefully.

"I think it's good faith. I think what I feel is true, not just that the grass is greener. Like I said, it's this unspoken feeling, something I just know she feels, too," Rob said. "But now I'm in a state of confusion. What do I do now? How does this affect me and my life, and the choices I've already made? I'm not saying that I should never have been ordained, my God, no. All I've ever wanted was to celebrate the Mass and work with people and serve the Lord. But think about it—I was only twenty-three when I was ordained. At twenty-three, what did I know?"

"I was twenty-seven myself."

"At twenty-three, most guys are out drinking and partying and getting their foot in the door of some company." Rob tried to explain his frustration. "When I see couples that age who want to marry, it makes me nervous. I take extra time with them; make them follow the Engaged Encounter program, just to ensure that they're ready. Because they're so naive at that age, so idealistic. At twenty-three, I was self-absorbed, full of this romantic Bing Crosby vision of myself as Father Rob. I was a fool."

"We all were." Father Anselm smiled wryly.

"On top of that, I was still broken up about Shannon. You remember? So how could I make an eternal promise, how could I pledge myself to God forever, and not know that she would come to me, appear in my life like an apparition, and make me feel something like—regret?" Rob swallowed hard against the rawness of his throat.

"Robert, you have the seven-year itch." The old priest tapped his nose in recognition. "It's been seven years, right?"

"Six."

"Ah, you're early." Father Anselm laughed gently. "We all go through this. This girl's a passing thing. Hang on, son, you'll make it." He lowered his voice, although no one could hear them in the confines of the confessional. "You can always, you know, do a little manual labor." He grinned at the younger priest.

Rob couldn't conspire. *This is my life, not a dirty joke.* "Yeah, or roll in the snow like St. Francis? I know. That's a given in this job, Father." He paused, and then plunged ahead. "But there's more."

"Go on."

"You know how the Bishop transferred me to the Chancery."

"Yes."

"Do you know why?"

Father Anselm shook his head. "I never heard."

"Because some of my fellow priests thought I was fooling around with her. I swear on my father's grave, nothing ever happened. But they took something totally out of context, a completely innocent breakfast in a public place, and blew it out of proportion. Then they called me a liar and wouldn't believe me when I tried to explain. Then one of them, my best friend —." He stopped, his fist held to his mouth.

Father Anselm watched in silent sympathy.

When he could speak again, Rob continued. "My best friend didn't believe me and went to the Bishop with a story. And suddenly the rug is yanked out from under me. They pull me out of the parish and throw me into the Chancery, into the canon law track, where I suppose I'll be until I die. I have to go to Rome, go back to school for years and read all this canon law. It's so sterile, so cold. I hate it; I really do. Maybe there's a form of ministry there, some sense of healing in annulments, but for me, there's nothing but papers and laws and files. I might as well work at a bank or an insurance company. Where are the people? What I want doesn't matter to the Bishop; I have no say in my own future. Everyone thinks I'm a hazard, that I might jump ship or something."

Rob stopped. He rubbed his hand across his unshaven face, shaking his head. "Father, you know what it's like. You've been in almost fifty years now."

"My golden jubilee is next year."

"Don't you ever get lonely?"

"I think that's one of the hazards of the job," Father Anselm acknowledged. "But there's always Jesus Christ, son. God is with us always. I'm never alone, and neither are you."

Rob blinked back the sudden wave of emotion that rolled through him. "I know that. *I know.* That's what makes it so difficult. I know I was called to be a priest. It was written in my heart. 'In my mother's womb You called me.' I don't question that. But was I called to celibacy? Was I called to be alone, separate from human touch, from the love and companionship of a woman? What if I was called to married life, too? When I was ordained, I made a promise that would affect my whole life. And now, I'm not sure that I can live by that anymore. It's not even the sex, Father—it's loneliness. Solitary confinement, even." His words sounded bitter to his own ears. "I can live without sex. But can I live the rest of my life without a companion? Or do I dare say—a wife?" The word hung in the air like a forbidden scent.

Father Anselm pulled off his glasses and rubbed them on a handkerchief. Rob saw the small blue cross embroidered in the corner. Finally the old priest spoke.

"I don't think I can help, Robert, really, I can't. I know you have a strong vocation. I saw it on your face, a young boy, your face shining like a cherub when you served at Mass, when you worked for me all those afternoons, all those summer vacations. I knew you were meant to be a priest, you without a father and your mother so—well, we know what she's like. I tried to help you as best I could. But I can't help you now, son. You can't have it both ways."

"I know."

"It's black or white with us, you know that. 'Thou art a priest forever,' says the Scripture. But if you step outside the gate, you can't come back. If you marry her—or someone else, whoever—you're not only out, you're excommunicated. Cut off forever from God. No sacraments. You can't even be buried in a Catholic cemetery. Unless you ask Rome for a laicization. Then you become just an ordinary Joe again. Not a priest, just a guy. Just a warm body at Mass. See what I mean? It's all or nothing. You're in or you're out; you're a priest or you're married."

"It's not right," Rob said softly, but with growing conviction.

"Well, that's the way it is, son," said Father Anselm bluntly. "We don't have a married clergy; we haven't had that since the Borgia popes. And I don't see it coming again soon."

"Yeah, I know. St. Peter had a wife, but it's not good enough for Rome today."

Father Anselm frowned. "You're sounding bitter now, Robert. That's not a good sign. It's only a step from that to loss of faith, son." Then he sighed. "You didn't come to me for answers. I think you know in your heart what you're going to do. I don't know what else to tell you, except good luck. And please God, make the right decision."

"I wish I knew what that was." Rob rose. "I'd better get going, Father. I'm due at my mom's for dinner tonight. Lord have mercy." He put out his hand to the old priest. "Thank you, Father."

Father Anselm pulled him into a paternal hug. "God bless you, son. Take care."

CHAPTER THIRTY-NINE

"Jessica, it's Rob."

"*Father* Rob?" In the context of her book-lined cubicle, her stacks of manuscripts and correspondence with authors, the priest's voice on the telephone was incongruous. She swung away from the computer screen. "It's good to hear your voice! How are you?"

"All right." He didn't sound quite all right, but what did she know? "How about you?"

"I'm fine. Working hard, as usual. Guess what?" Jessica bounced on her seat, glad to tell her news. "I got a promotion."

"Fantastic! Promoted to what, publisher?"

"Very funny. No, to marketing assistant. I just found out today. How funny that you called—good timing!"

"Yeah."

There was a long pause. Say something, she thought.

"Do you want to go out and celebrate?" he said. "That is, if you don't have plans already." He cleared his throat. "We could, you know, have dinner." His voice was edgy, nervous, so unlike the confident priest she remembered.

"Are you asking me out? Like on a date? Isn't there a rule against that, Father?" She laughed, too heartily; *don't get your hopes up.*

"We do get to eat, you know," he said with a spark of his old humor. "There's nothing wrong with having dinner with a friend."

"Tongues will wag, Father." She was only half-joking. Was dinner out with a priest, even just as friends, really all right?

"You have no idea," he said. "But I'm serious. Are you free tomorrow night?"

"I am, actually." Her needlepoint could wait.

"How about I pick you up at seven?"

"Okay. I'll see you then." Jessica hung up and put her chin on her hand. She was torn between elation and guilt. Nothing wrong with having dinner with one's priest and confessor, was there? Unless one was having erotic dreams about him? Oh, God, it was unthinkable. Incredible to even consider.

But Jessica suddenly didn't care. He was still a man, and she hadn't been out in months. Too much time alone with books and cats and needlepoint. Call this a faux date, then, a make-believe engagement with a safe and unavailable man. Maybe the act of dressing up and going out would jerk her from inertia, pull at the rusty gears, and set her rolling again. She needed to get back, as they said, into circulation again.

She picked at her cuticles on the train ride home, self-consciously tried to tame her auburn curls in the reflection of the window.

At home, she swished hangers across the pole, determined to find the right clothes. Nothing red, nothing sexy, nothing with cleavage, just a combination of garments that placed her in the moderate haven somewhere between strumpet and frump.

She spent Saturday in a self-conscious haze, unable to resist the mirror, the tiny zit on her chin, the unruliness of her awful hair. As the clock ticked toward seven, she pulled on a simple black dress, tied a printed chiffon scarf around her neck, and fastened her hair in a loose knot with a couple of sparkly clips. Never mind. She wasn't out to win any beauty pageants anyway. It was just a practice run.

When she opened the door, Rob stood in pressed khakis and a white shirt, his tie knotted just right, and a tweed jacket over his arm, very unpriestly indeed. She held open the door, unsure if she should ask him—a priest, a man! —inside her apartment, or if keeping him out would be rude. She hesitated.

But Rob smiled. "Your carriage awaits, milady," he said. Relieved, she followed him to his Jeep.

The stars shone white in an inky sky as they walked into the restaurant. A young hostess in a ruffled turquoise Mexican dress showed them to a table. Mariachi music strummed a lively background, and as they seated themselves, a half-dozen waiters and waitresses bearing a birthday cupcake swooped through the room, singing loudly in Spanish. They stopped at a table nearby. The birthday girl, a young teen with her family, blushed fiercely and hid her face. The singers finished with a shout, "*Olé!*" The diners applauded politely for the girl.

Jessica smiled as she clapped, and Rob leaned forward in his chair. "It's nice to see you smile. You know, you don't smile much."

Jessica stopped, self-conscious again. "Yes, I do. Don't I?"

"Not too often. But it's nice to see it." He picked up his menu. "What looks good to you?"

As he looked down the menu, Jessica peeked at him again. Something was different about him tonight. Maybe it was the secular environment of a Mexican restaurant. But he seemed more real to her, less priest and more man. He wasn't the same priest who had left St. Justin Martyr a few weeks before.

A waiter came and took their order, then brought margaritas in frosty goblets rimmed with salt. Jessica wiped the salt away from one side before taking the first sip. Its chill filled her mouth and sent a sharp pain to her forehead. She shivered, and then looked at Rob.

"I always forget how cold these are," he said, rubbing his forehead. "Congratulations on your promotion, Jess." He raised his glass to her.

"Thank you." Their glasses clinked softly.

"Tell me about your new job."

"Oh, it's great," Jessica said. "It's a good career move for me. I'll get to work with the marketing staff instead of just filing and sending rejection letters to authors. I'll get to go to the big publishing festivals in L.A., in New York, Miami, Chicago. Maybe even Frankfurt. I start next week."

"It sounds like a dream job."

"For me, it is." She couldn't help but notice his wistful tone. Jessica picked at the salt on her glass rim. "So how's your new assignment going?"

"They're keeping me busy." He didn't elaborate. "Isn't your publisher the one that did the nun's book, *Ordination and* whatever-it-is?"

"*Ordination, Not Subordination,*" Jessica corrected. "Patrice DuLac is the author. Yes, that's ours. It's selling like mad. We're into our second printing; that's unheard of for a small publisher like us. Hope—she's the publisher—she's ecstatic. She's planning to start a whole line of feminist and pop-theology books." Jessica took a tiny sip of her margarita. The tart lime slush melted in her mouth. "Have you read it?"

Rob shook his head. "I've been busy. It sounds kind of flaky. Isn't it?"

"As a matter of fact, it's not. Maybe I'm just a new-born Catholic," she smiled, "but I have to say that a lot of her ideas have merit. Why shouldn't we ordain women? Why shouldn't women have a bigger say in the Church?"

"I agree, actually," Rob said. "I have no problem with the ordination of women. There are other issues that are more pressing to me personally, but I would welcome that. Why not?"

"You should read her book. I have a copy at home. I'll lend it to you."

"Thanks, I'd like that."

The waiter brought their plates, steaming hot platters of rolled tacos, chicken enchiladas, tender beans and rice.

"Mmm, I love this." Rob savored the melting cheese of his enchilada. "I was raised on it, you know."

"I thought you were Portuguese."

"I am. But where I grew up, where my mom still lives, is right in a Mexican neighborhood. *Taquerías* on every corner. Tortillas help build strong bodies twelve ways, you know."

Jessica swallowed a bite. "I didn't discover real Mexican food until I moved to the City. Growing up, what we called tacos was a handful of corn chips with ground beef on top. We'd dress it up with tomatoes and sour cream, but salsa never even crossed our minds. It was very middle class. Very white bread and mayonnaise, if you know what I mean."

"It wasn't bad, though, was it?"

"No, it was fine; I had a decent childhood and plenty of opportunities. I just got kind of sideswiped when I tried to make it in the Big City." She pushed her plate away, half of the food uneaten. "I'm stuffed. I can't eat any more."

Rob placed his knife and fork on his own empty plate and folded his napkin, his face unreadable to her. She carefully folded her napkin like his and waited for the thing he must need to say. There had to be another reason for him to have called her, and asked her out on this whatever-it-was, non-date.

"Jess, what do you see yourself doing in about five years?"

She blinked in surprise. "Me? I don't know. Married, I would hope, with a baby. Working somewhere, maybe working at home. Nothing too adventurous."

"Oh." Rob fidgeted with his napkin, pulling on a loose thread of the cotton weave. "You're seeing someone now?" He stumbled over his words, as if embarrassed. "I don't mean to pry. I just didn't know you had a boyfriend."

"No, no, I'm not dating anyone." She picked at her own napkin's threads. "I really haven't been on the market, so to speak. It was just too traumatic after all that I went through. I've been thinking about it lately, and I think I'm ready to try again." But that was too suggestive. Jessica tried to amend her statement. "I mean, I'm open to the idea."

"I'm sorry," Rob said, exasperated. "This isn't coming out right. Nothing is coming out the way I planned."

"I don't understand."

"Do you want to know what my new assignment is really like?" he asked. "It's horrible. It's like working in exile. Siberia. I'm so cut off from my old life. I really miss St. Justin. I really miss—people like you." He kept his eyes down on the loose thread, twisting it around and around his finger.

People like me.

"Everyone tells me it's just a rough patch, that I'll get used to it. I know it's only been a few weeks. But somehow everything has changed for me. It's complicated. Too complicated for words."

Rob yanked the loose thread from the napkin, breaking it. He looked at Jessica. "I'm thinking about leaving."

Jessica felt bound to his gaze, the brown eyes locked to her green ones. Infinite possibilities. Impossible dreams. *My God.* She swallowed hard.

"Leaving." She said the word carefully, as if formed in glass. "Leaving the priesthood?"

"I haven't decided to do it yet. I'm just thinking." He broke his gaze and looked around the dining room. "I mean, really, it's too big a decision to take lightly. It's like a divorce. But more so—it's really, really ugly, and really, really permanent."

"Your new job is that bad?"

"Yes and no. It's not that the job is bad or unworthy, it's that they forced me to take it against my will, and that I have no say in my future. They don't trust me, for some reason, and my friends all think I'm some kind of Romeo." He hesitated, and then said, "Because I had breakfast with you that one time."

"Because of me?"

"No, because of me. See, I left the seminary halfway through because I fell in love with a woman. We were going to get married, but it didn't work out; I couldn't deny my vocation. I had to crawl on my belly like a worm, but they let me back in. Since then, there's been this little black mark next to my name, like, 'Watch out for Souza, he's high-risk.' It doesn't matter that I've been totally faithful to my vocation, that I've never once given them any real reason to question me." He looked around the room as if scouting spies, then back to her.

"But it's also bad timing. There was another priest, a friend of mine, who just left in a scandal over a woman, and then when someone saw us having breakfast together in March, they jumped to conclusions. I've been falsely accused, and I can't prove myself innocent. It's such a witch-hunt," he said.

She wasn't sure where he was going. "But if you leave, you'll just be proving them right, won't you?"

"Maybe," he said. "But *I* would know the difference, even if they didn't."

"Then you wouldn't be a priest anymore." Not Father. Just Rob.

"No, that's not quite right. I'll be a priest forever. But I couldn't perform the sacraments, like say Mass or do weddings. It would be like ripping myself in half, Jess. I'm a priest to the core. It's an eternal mark on my soul."

It hurt to watch the pain on his face, to hear the emotion catch in his voice. She felt as if she were seeing him for the first time, seeing him with no protective layer, naked in his anguish.

"But how can I go on when there's this suspicion and doubt about my character? About my vocation?"

There was no answer she could give. Jessica listened as sympathetically as she could, her mind racing along with his, to whatever conclusion he had reached.

"And yet, at the same time, there's this other part of me that says, 'Time is slipping away, you're getting older, and you'll be trapped here forever, bitter and alone.' I have faith in my vocation, Jess, but I think celibacy is wrong." Rob hesitated, his eyes focused on the tabletop, like granite or steel, a harder stare than she'd ever seen. "I think I was also called to married life."

The mariachi music rollicked in the background. Silverware rattled and glasses clinked. The clamor of voices in the restaurant roared in her ears. She forced a response from her clamped chest. "So what are you going to do, then?"

"I don't know yet." He looked at her then, brown eyes like circles of dark polished wood. "It all depends."

"On what?"

He took a deep breath and said, "On a lot of things. On you."

She closed her eyes. Her hands shook in her lap, tight fists. She felt as if her world were rocking beneath her, as if the ground had shifted and she might slip through to some other life, some other existence. *Oh, yes, my God, but not like this.*

"Rob," she said, for the first time, not Father, just Rob. "You can't leave for me." Tears welled in her eyes. "You can't. I can't be the reason that you leave. I just barely survived this other thing." The tears began to roll down her face.

"Jess, I—"

"Wait." She dabbed at her eyes with her napkin, ignoring the troubled glance of the waiter as he passed. "I'll be totally honest with you, Rob. I have feelings for you. More than you know. But it doesn't matter. You're a priest. No matter how I feel, you're *married*. You're married to the Church and we can't get into that kind of a relationship."

He tried to speak, but she insisted, "No, let me finish, please." She wiped her eyes again. "You don't know what you want. But you have to decide. I'm not going to make you any promises or tell you that I'll wait for you, wait for the divorce to be final. That wouldn't be fair to either of us. I can't tell you what to do or anything at all, because it's too big a decision to rest on me. You can't make it based on me." She covered her face with her hands, her cheeks hot to the touch.

"I'm sorry, Jessica," his eyes cast down, voice chastened. "I didn't mean to put you in this position. I shouldn't have said anything. I'm sorry." He waved to the waiter. "Let's go."

Jessica took her purse and went to the restroom while he paid the bill. She looked at herself in the mirror, carroty hair, brown freckles dotting her cheeks, red-rimmed eyes like a rabbit's. Her mind was whirling. *He wants me, he might even love me, but I can't get into this. It's too sticky, too complicated.* She pressed cool, damp paper towels to her eyes.

Outside, Jessica looked up at the brightness of the stars. She felt Rob's nearness, felt the flush of warmth when he brushed past her, opening the car door for her. She smelled the clean scent of his cologne and the leathery smell of his car. She couldn't think of anything to say on the short ride to her apartment.

He walked her to her apartment door. She put her key into the lock and opened the door.

"Jess, I'm sorry for upsetting you."

"I know." She smiled to show that she wasn't angry. *Go on, nail the coffin lid down.* "But I meant it. You can't base your decision on me. I will not take you away from the priesthood, no matter what I might want."

"I'm a grown man, Jess," he said softly, his tone sure. "If I left, it would be because I wanted to, not because you enticed me away, or trapped me in your web." He smiled a little. "It's nothing like that at all."

"Yes, but that's what people will think. That's what they'll say." Pointing fingers and long, cruel stares. "And what if you left to be with me, and then it didn't work out? What if we hated each other after a month? Or a year, or ten years? You would always have a secret accusation in your heart, that I made you leave, that you gave up that wonderful priestly life for me. And you would resent me. You would. I can't be responsible for that."

"You wouldn't be responsible."

"You might feel differently then, though." She moved to go inside. "Whatever you do, whatever decision you make, you have to make it alone. But I can't be part of it."

His face looked haggard and dark in the porch light. She only wanted to run her fingers along his cheek, to feel the scratch of his shadow under her fingertips, to trace the softness of his lips, to hear him whisper into her hair. She knew she could have it with a word, a gesture.

"I don't think we should see each other or even talk until you've resolved this," she said. "If you decide to stay in, then God bless you. You're a wonderful priest." Her voice choked. "If you decide, for whatever reasons, that you can't be a priest anymore, maybe we'll talk. But I can't do it any other way. It's too much."

"I understand." He gestured with his hand, half-extended it to her, but she couldn't take it. "I'm sorry, Jess."

"Thanks for dinner. Goodbye." She left him outside, closed the door behind her and leaned against it, wracked with the release of tears.

CHAPTER FORTY

Rob stood in the stairway of the diocesan offices chatting with a reporter from *The Catholic Monitor*, the diocesan newspaper whose office was located in the basement.

"Do you know anyone who can write? We need some help here on the paper," the reporter said. The three-man news staff—a priest and two laypeople—had recently suffered a flood of letters to the publisher—Bishop Cornelius—for and against the nun's book on ordination.

"Long hours and low pay, right?" Rob joked.

"Of course!"

"I'll let you know if I think of anyone." Rob glanced at the clock on the wall and started back up the stairs to the Chancery Office. Halfway up, he thought about Lawrence, and how Therese, who fancied herself a writer, had so tormented his friend. Even though they weren't talking, Rob still wanted to help. He called after the reporter, telling him Therese's name.

Down in the foyer again, Rob was distracted by the sight of a crowd gathering outside the glass double doors, what might even be called an angry crowd.

Young women, some with children, older women, some quite elderly, women of every age stood outside in the heat of the early summer sun. Many carried signs: "Stop Silencing Women's Voices," "Ordain Womyn NOW!" "Sister Patrice – Martyr," "Jesus wouldn't do this!" Priests and lay workers gathered in the foyer to watch the crowd beyond the glass doors.

Someone outside began to chant, and soon more voices joined together. Their chant seeped in through the glass. "Ordination, not subordination!

Ordination, not subordination!" The protesters formed a circle and marched in time to the chant. "Ordination, not subordination!"

"What the hell's going on?" a priest asked.

"Bunch of housewives and lesbos want to be ordained," said another.

"On account of that nun's book?"

"Fine kettle of *fish*," cracked someone, to laughter.

The receptionist's desk was surrounded by priests looking out the shaded glass windows. She stood up.

"You guys just don't get it, do you?" She removed her headset and pushed through the men, opened the glass door and walked out.

The chant of the protesters flashed loudly into the foyer, then muted as the door closed. The receptionist was met with stares from the marchers, which turned to cheers as she joined them. More people gathered outside on the cement steps, spilling down the sidewalk. The chants grew louder.

Rob wriggled back from the window and moved toward the stairs to his office. He had papers on his desk that he had no interest in. The protest amused him—a little rabble-rousing might make things interesting—though he wisely kept his face impartial. He still hadn't read that book, hadn't had time, and hadn't wanted to after the debacle with Jessica. He still cringed, remembering. *How could I be so insensitive? So presumptuous?* He leaned against the stair railing, above the heads of the crowds inside and out, watching through the glass. Remarks drifted up from the gallery below.

"Don't burn the book! Roast the author!"

"How many women will ever be priests? 'Nun!'"

Rob didn't see any reason why women shouldn't be ordained. He had known nuns who were far priestlier than he was. But he didn't foresee any great change coming, not this century. Maybe in the next, but Rob wouldn't be around to see it.

The crowd outside was growing, and their chant grew louder with it. "Let us in! Let us in!"

"Do you hear that? Let us *sin!*" someone joked below him.

Two vans drove up, with large news insignia on their sides. News teams scrambled from the vans, with cameras and microphones. The protesters chanted with new vigor and brandished their placards for the cameras. Rob wondered what the Bishop thought, upstairs in his episcopal sanctum, the courtyard full of protesters visible from the window.

Jessica got out of Hope's car and shut the door. Hope wanted to see the protest for herself, and she had grabbed Jessica from the marketing department, saying, "You're the resident Catholic. You come along, too."

On the way over, they heard updates on the radio. "City police are now diverting traffic from the main boulevard at the Catholic Church's diocesan offices. Drivers are urged to take alternate routes to the downtown area."

Jessica and Hope parked as close as they could, still several blocks away, and then walked until they could see the crowds. News vans blocked the streets, along with police cars. The protesters marched in a circle, with many others crowding the sidewalks and street before the building. Yet the march was peaceful. The police officers were not even dressed in riot gear.

"Women hold up half the sky," shouted the marchers.

"Look at this crowd!" Hope shaded her eyes from the sun, trying to count. "There must be hundreds of people here. Maybe more. And the media—my God, we couldn't ask for better publicity. I should have brought books to sell!"

A cry rose up as three women left the diocesan building and joined the marchers. A minute later, the door opened again and another woman came out. The cheer was tremendous.

"Look, there's Sister Patrice!" Hope pointed. She hurried along the sidewalk, scooting among clusters of people, with Jessica behind her.

Sister Patrice, the author in question, was giving an interview to a TV crew. "Yes, I've been a Roman Catholic nun for thirty-five years. I have just taken a leave from my order, the Sisters of Hagia Sophia, to promote my book on a national tour." Patrice saw Hope. "Oh, here's my publisher now!"

Hope smoothed her hair before the camera turned to her.

"How have sales of *Ordination, Not Subordination* been?"

Hope smiled and gave the smooth response of one accustomed to public relations. "We're well through our second printing, and have ordered a third, larger printing to meet the demand. Vision Press is thrilled to have Sister Patrice DuLac as our premier author. She's a woman of courage and perception. A real champion for women's rights in the Church today."

Jessica watched from a few paces away.

From his vantage point on the stairs inside the building, Rob watched the event unfold like something on TV. He had seen a surge and heard the cheers when the author-nun showed up at the march. Every time someone broke ranks from within the diocese and stepped outside, the crowd cheered even more.

He became aware of a competing chant and realized that a second group had arrived. He could see a small cluster of placards above the heads of the crowd: "Catholics United for Tradition," "Jesus Didn't Ordain Women!" "God Bless Our MALE Priests." The women protesters chanted louder to drown out the counter-protest.

The self-righteous counter-protesters irritated Rob. They were the same kind of Catholics who wanted a reversal of all the changes of Vatican II: a return to the Latin Mass, nuns back in their habits, and priests like gods among peasants. Rob thought about going outside himself, decided against it, and thought about it again, as the discord grew. A canon lawyer passed him on the stairs.

"Better come up, Rob. There are marriages to unmake, you know."

"Yeah, I know." But he stayed where he was, tired of watching, yet reluctant to lock himself into the staid Chancery office while the excitement went on. *I just want to get out of here.* Outside, the vast blue of the summer sky beckoned, and the trees moved gently as with a small breeze. He walked down the steps. At the glass door, someone grabbed his arm.

"You're not going out there, are you?"

"I just need some air."

"Don't be a fool. You're committing suicide."

"I know." The hand released his arm, and Rob stepped out through the glass doors. The sunshine was too bright in his eyes and he paused momentarily to shade the glare. The chant paused, the marchers saw his black clerical shirt, his white dog collar, and a huge cheer went up. Rob was surrounded by marchers, women and a few men, hands clapping around him.

"Bless you, Father!"

"Thanks for your support, Father!"

He was swept into the motion of the circle. Rob smiled sheepishly and took a self-conscious turn with the marchers. Toward the side he stepped out, away from the cameras and news crews. A reporter caught up with him.

"You're a Catholic priest—how do you feel about the ordination of women?"

"I believe that it's time the Church took a good long look at some of its old restrictions and practices. Some traditions are anachronistic. And others, well, they seem misguided in this day and age."

"Are you talking about women's ordination, or other issues facing the Church today?"

"Let's say I'm talking about women's ordination. But the same thought applies to other issues."

"Such as?"

"That's all I have to say at the moment."

Rob wanted to walk away, to get away from the noise and clear his head. He felt like he had to stay now, though; everyone thought he was such a champion of women's rights. He maneuvered through the crowd and filtered toward the back, toward the shade of a tree where the crowd was thin.

"Hi," she said at his elbow. He turned, his heart in his throat.

"Jess! Oh, your famous author, right?"

"Right." Jessica pointed to Patrice in the crowd. "There she is." She spoke as if they had never had that dinner conversation. "That was brave of you, coming out like that to support her."

"No, it wasn't really. I'm not brave at all. I'm a coward and a fool. But that's neither here nor there, is it?" He tugged at his high collar. Sweat beaded his brow.

She didn't say anything. Just looked at him in his clerical suit, then away. *I'm not a man, just a priest, as bitter and lonely as Shannon said I'd be.* He watched the profile of Jessica's freckled face, the russet tint of her lips, and how the breeze tossed the curls on her shoulders, coiled strands the color of old pennies in a jar.

From his office up on the second floor, Bishop Paul Cornelius watched the marchers who snaked around the building now; saw which of his people left the walled sanctum of the building, observed the priest and the woman talking under the blossoming tree. *Don't do it, Rob,* he thought. *Don't do it!*

CHAPTER FORTY-ONE

Rob drove straight from the protest at the diocese to a bookstore down on the waterfront and bought himself a copy of the infamous book. Then he went home to his room, kicked off his black shoes, and lay in his clerical clothes on his bed with the book. Jessica had been involved with its creation. She had recommended that he read it. She had read it herself. It was almost like holding her in her hands. Those were adolescent reasons to buy a book, but he didn't care, turning past the cover and a page of acknowledgments to the introduction.

The nun's feminist viewpoint intrigued him. Rob read on, engaged by the nun's offbeat yet scholarly contentions until he finished. He had anticipated her conclusion and enjoyed some of her arguments, especially after seeing the author in person at the protest. He hadn't expected more than that. But certain lines from the nun's treatise kept coming back to him.

> *Why can't a married priest celebrate the Eucharist? Because the taint of Womyn clings to him.*

Her words resonated. They prickled at him like slivers, a painful jab when he brushed across them in his mind. Sister hadn't intended for this to be an emancipation proclamation for priests, he thought. Far from it.

Rob arose from his creaking bed and stretched. The day was long gone, a moon on the rise outside his window. He saw its blurry orb through bubbled glass. He had missed dinner, lying on his bed, turning pages until he'd consumed the entire volume, but he wasn't hungry. The night loomed before him, humid, too sultry for June. Tomorrow was another empty Saturday.

Mandatory celibacy is an abuse of human rights.

He tried to open the window but it was painted shut, long years ago. He cursed it under his breath but it remained stuck fast. Rob walked to the mirror above the dresser and unbuttoned his clerical shirt, wrinkled from hours of wear. He flipped open the buckle of his belt, the gold-toned buckle that the Knights of Columbus at St. Justin had given him, and let his trousers slip to the floor.

…a clerical caste system that excludes some because of gender or marital status.

He pulled off his white cotton undershirt and black socks; saw himself, a reflection of a priest in boxer shorts, his small gold crucifix hanging naked above his heart, against his chest. What was the measure of his devotion? He offered himself to God, his lean brown body, his open hands, his bare skin like the secret underside of his chalice: only for God to see.

He felt himself standing as at a fork in a road. Rob looked at the few strands of gray that had already appeared in his dark hair. He looked at his face, the smudges of bruise beneath his eyes a mark of his Portuguese heritage, dark eyes that stared back with equal intensity. He began to look old to himself, middle-aged already at thirty; he had felt ancient since birth, with two aged parents. And now he knew himself cursed by them, too; he felt his spirit turning black and sour. He could hear himself on the telephone these days with the same bleak tone that his mother always used, nothing that could make her happy, would ever satisfy her. And here he was, netted in the same trap, melancholic, choleric, stubborn, his path mapped out by others, his road rutted with disappointment. His life felt lived already.

One bright spot illuminated his day. Jessica had been glad to see him, he was sure. She hadn't known he would be there, and he had certainly never expected the protest to take place. Such a chance meeting. Such a brief opportunity.

She pointed out Sister Patrice from a distance, and they stood together without talking under the shade of the tree near the steps, watching the spectacle. Bees buzzed in the white blossoms above their heads, and a bird rustled in the leaves. The chanting of the protesters grew louder and the crowd continued to swell. Summer sunshine flooded the scene with golden light. But under the shade of the small tree, it was cool and sweetly scented.

Jessica raked her loose hair from her face, twined a finger in the corkscrew of a rusty curl. "Have you decided what to do?" she asked, her words light, her eyes focused on the crowd.

"Not yet."

She flicked a glance at him with a quirk of her mouth, twirling the curl tight on her finger. Her nails were lightly varnished with a soft apricot color that matched her lips. Her sleeveless pale blue dress somehow gave her the look of a young mother. They stood under the tree, Rob sweating in his severe black clericals, until Jessica's boss waved at her to come.

"I have to go. There's Hope." She smiled at him. "It was good to see you again. A nice surprise."

"Just lucky coincidence," Rob said. He wanted to embrace her, but he put his hands into his pockets. "Take care."

Jessica walked away from him and the tree, the crowd and the media, left him alone at the steps of the diocese, his virtue intact.

In his room, the memory replayed itself. He should have said something else. *Be patient, Jess. Wait for me. I have to be sure.* He feared failing her, afraid to give the world outside another try. What if he couldn't make it out there as a man, as a husband and a father? He didn't even have a job or know where to look. *I don't know what else to do but this, but minister, serve the people, lead the worship. I'm trapped if I stay, and if I leave, I'm doomed.*

Rob turned from the mirror and knelt on the cool floor to pray.

Ordinary Time

CHAPTER FORTY-TWO

At the Church of the Resurrection, Father Lawrence Poole packed his good clothes, his linen slacks, white shirts, silk ties, casual designer comfort for his vacation. Two weeks in Italy would do him good. And this time, he didn't have to worry about cutting corners. The check from the recording company, even with the fat cut the agent took, assured Lawrence that this trip would be anything but budget.

Lawrence looked forward to two weeks in the Roman sun. He could smell the Tiber River in his mind, hear the wail of Italian sirens up the cobbled streets, E flat-A natural, could practically taste the fruity olive oil of a green almost peridot in hue. Lawrence sang his *Exsultet* under his breath as he packed. "Rejoice, Heavenly powers." Two weeks away, then back, bang, into the studio; imagine, a studio full of musicians to back him up, to work under his command, playing the music he himself created. They had two months to record the work before the liturgical seasons began to demand his attention again. Lawrence would commute to the city studios from Resurrection, and he didn't even mind having to stay in the parish, because everything had changed here.

Therese was gone. She had taken a position at the *Catholic Monitor*, raking up a little muck in the diocese (a very little, under the watchful eye of the Bishop), and would no longer haunt the premises. And what was even better than that, Lawrence's pastor, Tom Connors himself, had been transferred. Lawrence hadn't realized that Tom's term was almost up. But suddenly Resurrection had a new pastor, an older priest about 55 years old, a traditionalist with a progressive mind; he and Lawrence worked well together already. Lawrence remained as associate, with permission from the Bishop to continue to pursue his music.

So many times Lawrence had wanted to call Rob, to try to break the ice between them, to share his good news. But he hadn't done it yet. He felt aphasic, unable to make an apology for an act he felt was intrinsically, morally correct. And yet he knew what he had done to his best friend. *Et tu, Brute?*

Lawrence counted socks and silky briefs from a bureau drawer and packed them into the suitcase. *I did it because I care. Because I love you and I didn't want to lose you.* But Rob was lost to him now, anyway, so what was the point? Maybe when he came back from Italy, maybe when he'd finished the recording sessions. Then tempers would have cooled, and maybe Rob would be ready, would want to hear from him again.

Lawrence hummed under his breath as he finished packing.

At St. Perpetua, Father William Fairlie spoke with a potential new choir director. The young man had just graduated from college with a music degree, he had all kinds of ideas, and he was just so enthusiastic. William watched him speak, noting the dear little cowlick at the top of his shapely head, the way the boy pushed at his glasses when they slipped, and the lovely timbre of the voice. You can wake me with a song any morning, dear, William thought. *Rise and shine!*

William approved of the black jeans the young one wore, and the way they fit, accenting the trim waist, yet hugging the derriere. William looked again at the neatly printed resume, noted correct spelling and an appealing use of fonts. "You're hired," he said, shaking the young man's hand with a firm grasp.

Lead us not into temptation.

In his office down at the diocese, Bishop Paul Cornelius finished a telephone call to his classmate, a dean at Catholic University in Washington D.C.

The Chancellor rapped at the door and came in. "You wanted to see me?"

"Yes, hi, Fred. I just talked with that friend of mine at Catholic U. and they're holding a place for Rob Souza. You'd better get after the boy and get him to sign the admission papers."

"I think it's taken care of already," the Chancellor said.

"He's ready to go?"

"I imagine so. He filled them out and signed them last week. He needs a challenge. He's not too happy down the hall with us."

"No? Well, that'll change. You'd better tell him to buy some snow boots and a parka. It's colder than a brass monkey back there in winter," the Bishop said, recalling childhood days of snow forts and salty sidewalks, nostalgia coating his memories like hoarfrost.

"I'll tell him. When should he leave?"

The Bishop calculated aloud. "Hmm. The term starts in September. He can leave his books and such at St. Joan's. He'll stay in the residence hall at C.U. with the other priests; there's a room for him already." The Bishop squinted at his liturgical desk calendar, leather bound, executive edition. "Tell him to book a flight for mid-August. He can use the time to settle in. Make himself at home. How's that?" he asked the Chancellor.

"That should work. He'll be fine there. A change of scenery and all that."

"Yes. I'm sure it's just what he needs."

At St. Ambrose, Father Phil Lacaro closed the avocado-green refrigerator door. He had gazed into the cold for a solid five minutes, fighting his desire to seize the nearest delicious morsel. No matter if it was just a shriveled celery stalk or a crumbling slice of American cheese. He wouldn't have cared. His stomach ached, his hands trembled with hunger. But he was trying to cut back, no, officially diet, really control his appetite for once. His doctor had told him that his diabetes was out of control, and now Phil had to take insulin shots morning and evening and test his own blood sugar every day. His sore fingers were red and pricked.

Phil hated the whole thing, hated the diet, the diabetes, even his doctor. He was trying to be good. But it didn't hurt to look at the food, did it? Ah, never mind. He had to get going anyway. The bar clock on the wall, the big red Hamm's logo that looked like the waterfall was really flowing, read four o'clock. He took his keys from the walnut burl coffee table. Time to go. Phil had agreed to act as chaplain for the Catholic Boy Scouts troops, at least temporarily. He didn't much care for children usually. They didn't do a thing for him. But who knows, this could be fun, he thought, spending a couple of hours hanging out with some kids every week.

At least they'll take my mind off food for a while. With a last yearning look at the refrigerator, Phil closed the rectory door behind him.

"You can put your clothes back on now, Father."

Father Hector Salvo looked at the doctor, startled. "What is it? Can you tell?"

The young doctor washed his hands at a small sink in the corner of the examination room. Hector watched the hand-washing method approvingly, even as he waited for the bad news.

"It's a simple skin rash. It's totally harmless. Uncomfortable, I know, but it'll go away by itself in a few weeks."

"But the lesions—I thought it must be —." He couldn't say what he'd really thought.

"What, poison oak? No, it's just a rash. Nothing serious, I hate to disappoint you," the doctor smiled. "Go ahead and get dressed and I'll write up a prescription for the itching. And try not to scratch." He left the room.

Hector pulled on his clerical shirt and black pants. The room had chilled him; now he would surely get a cold on top of the horrid skin disease. It couldn't be a simple rash. Such red sores couldn't be less than a symptom of something worse. Leukemia. Melanoma. AIDS. He buttoned his shirt up to the neck. A knock at the door startled him.

"Okay, Father," the doctor popped his head in. "Here's the prescription. Just a little cortisone cream. 'Use as needed to relieve itching.' Okay?"

Hector took the square of paper from the doctor's hand. He gave what he hoped was a smile; the doctor waved and closed the door. Cortisone cream! That was a laugh. Can't cure cancer with a topical. Hector squirmed, trying not to itch. He grudgingly folded the paper in half, into quarters, then eighths, slid it into his pocket. Well, he'd give it a try for a week. If the rash wasn't gone by then, Hector would be back.

No doctor's going to tell me I'm not sick!

At St. Cecile, Father Cesar Castro tore the last check from the account book. All bills paid, all accounts settled, and money left in the bank. Cesar checked the balance again. It was a satisfyingly large number; a soft cushion for St. Cecile's to fall back on during the summer when the collection usually dropped a bit. Cesar smiled to himself. It was good to be the pastor.

It was official now. Monsignor Grimmley was gone, retired to the seminary guesthouse, his petit point and dahlias and short temper gone with him. Well, not the dahlias. They were leafy and green out front of the rectory, their yellow and pink and orange heads balled up, ready to explode like fireworks of soft color. Come to think of it, dahlias were quite pretty. None of the other parishes had such pretty specimens in front.

Maybe I should read a book on how to care for them, so they do not dry up and die. A pastor needs a hobby, he told himself. Something to occupy his off hours. Some priests got up to no good, left to their own devices. That convinced him. Tomorrow Cesar would go down to the bookstore and get some gardening books, maybe stop in at the garden center for supplies. He could get some gloves and a pair of knee-pads. A straw hat for the sun. One had to keep an eye on the parish. Keep up appearances, and such. Nothing worse than an ill-kempt rectory.

After all, people will talk.

Jessica fastened her seatbelt and settled herself for the flight. She looked out the window at the airport as passengers bustled past in the aisle. Heat rose in shimmering waves from the tarmac. From below she heard thumps and groans as the luggage was loaded. Her marketing manager, Isabel, slammed the overhead bin and plumped into the seat next to her with a sigh.

"I'll be glad when we get there."

"Me, too. I've never been to New York."

"Book shows are fun but exhausting. You'll really get to know the business this way," Isabel said. "If we have another hit like *Ordination*, we'll be in great shape this year. Maybe we can even go to the Frankfurt show in the fall."

The plane began to move and a young steward addressed the travelers over the speaker.

"Thank you for flying United Airlines, Flight 220. We'll be stopping in New York on our way to Italy this evening. Please fasten your seatbelts and stow all personal belongings in preparation for takeoff." He repeated the message in Italian, the words rolling from his tongue like a lover's vow.

Jessica flipped through the in-flight magazine. It fell open at its center to reveal a photographic advertisement for Italy. Jessica saw the gleaming white walls of the Vatican, the smiling figure of the Pope at his balcony; in another shot, priests walked in a double line down a wet cobbled street. Their faces glowed with some inner certitude, a deeper faith than she had yet discovered.

Jessica understood something of celibacy; she hadn't been physically intimate with a man for more than five years. But she had always known that sometime down the road, a man would come into her life, slip between her fears and memories. She couldn't conceive of a life without that sort of union in it. Jessica could never have imagined that the man to kindle her soul would be a priest. And without even trying, she had done the same for him.

She wouldn't think about him now. It hurt to think of missed opportunities and a romance that would never come to fruition. She believed that he cared for her, that he was confused, but more than anything, that he would stay a priest. She flipped the page of the magazine and saw Big Ben, a red double-decker bus, the glory of England in beautiful color photographs. She had her whole life ahead of her. The right man would find her somehow.

The engines roared to life, and Jessica felt a surge of nervous excitement as the plane accelerated for takeoff.

CHAPTER FORTY-THREE

In late June, on the feast of the Holy Trinity, Rob arrived at Holy Trinity Cathedral for the year's ordinations. As instructed in the invitation, over his black clericals he wore a simple white alb with a red stole, the color for the feast day. He parked his car on the street and walked up the cathedral steps, brushing past the memory of Jessica, her hair blowing in the gray wind, trying desperately to say and unsay words that should never have passed between them. He joined the line of priests, waiting for the music to begin.

Ordinations gave Rob more than a sense of *déjà vu*; he felt time-warped, as if it were his own ordination six years before. He might have been one of the seminarians waiting to walk up the aisle with his parents, except Rob's father was dead; his mother and brother had escorted him. He could remember every detail of his ordination the way some people, he supposed, remembered the minutia of their wedding day.

Some of the music at their ordination had been Spanish, to honor Hector Salvo's Mexican heritage. Lawrence had composed a piece, and wanted to sing it, but the Director of Worship had convinced him not to perform at his own ordination. A musical friend from the seminary sang the piece instead, a haunting arrangement of Psalm 110, *Tu es sacerdoz in aeternum*. Thou are a priest forever. Rob had received a huge lei from his Hawaiian cousins the morning of his ordination to wear during the procession. The fragrance of white mai flowers filled his senses, an indelible scent-memory of the day. He had given the lei to his mother when he was called forward from the community to be ordained.

Today he walked in the double line of singing priests under the banners and swags, heard the reverberations of the organ, looked surreptitiously for the priests he had called friends. Lawrence was nowhere to be seen, nor Cesar. Rob spied Hector from a distance, and William, who winked and waved his pinkie finger as he passed. Rob gave a tight smile. Behind the priests, in came the Bishop and his master of ceremonies.

The liturgy began. Rob listened and watched, his eyes on the altar or following the words of the hymns in his program. The memory of the lei filled his head, the sweet, almost rotten scent, a long loop around his neck. The Bishop's voice, calling forth the candidates to the priesthood, might have been an echo from long ago, asking, "Are you resolved to consecrate your life to God, and to pledge yourself every day to Christ the High Priest, who offered himself as a perfect sacrifice?"

"I am, with God's help," came the answer.

"Do you promise to respect and obey me and my successors?"

"I do, with God's help."

No other promises in the rite. No other pledge to make or break. Every other oath was unspoken. No vow of poverty, but a living wage, yes, and a promise of celibacy, a life apart from that kind of union. It was understood. A given. No questions asked. Rob watched the four young men, their faces radiant, rejoicing.

I know how they feel, he thought. He had consecrated himself to the Church as an orphan binds himself to a loving foster family. But what if that love is conditional, a thin, hard line that he dare not cross? What kind of man does the rejected child become? *But you weren't a child; you were a man at twenty-three. You were called, and you answered. You believed in the Church. You married Her.* The old joke about marriage was who wants to live in an institution? The venerable cathedral and her contingent of priests, that which had once felt so enveloping and familial, seemed overwhelmingly claustrophobic.

And what was he now? A fatherless, childless man. Sexless. Priest.

The cathedral choir began the *Litany of Saints*.

"St. Michael."

Pray for us.

The four candidates lay on the floor of the cathedral in front of the assembly, prone before the altar in complete humility to the Lord.

"St. John the Baptist."

Pray for us.

Before the Church and the people, Rob thought, remembering the chill marble, his forehead pressed into his crossed arms, his nose half an inch from the floor.

"Saint Peter and Saint Paul."

Pray for us.

The music of the *Litany*, the Holy Spirit, had surrounded him as he had lain there, tears dripping from his eyes, praying, *thank You, God, thank You for this blessed day.*

"St. Lawrence."

Pray for us.

Rob prayed now, as he watched the prostrate men. *Oh Lord, how could I think of letting it go? How could I ever walk away from You?* He felt squeezed in two, as a cell dividing. His once integrated life pinched at the center, pulled in like a cincture, his two selves bubbling away from one another. *Here, my God life. There, my—what?*

What was real now was a cold and empty room three thousand miles away, classrooms and books and the study of a subject that bored him, jaded him, and numbed him to others' pain. And back here, what awaited him? His future planned in an office down the hall, an errant child with a tick mark next to his name. His devotion to RCIA, delivering new Catholics to a Church in desperate need of members, dismissed as risky. And by his friends, forsaken—Rob glanced down the rows of priests seated together, seeing faces but meeting no eyes, no conspiratorial wink. Deny me thrice, he thought.

The seminarians remained on the floor as the Bishop stepped forward to the microphone. "Pour upon your servants the Blessing of the Holy Spirit. We offer You these men for ordination: support them with your unfailing love."

Rob could have laughed, or wept, at the Bishop's words. The only loving support Rob had felt for weeks, for months, it seemed, was from Jessica. He had held her away when he knew of her feelings, tried to purge his mind of her, to fight his own desires and the suspicions of his peers. He admired her, for her strength through her rape and resurrection, her faith, her own precarious journey to Church, into an integrated life with Christ. And at his weakest, when he most wanted to leave the Church, she could have pulled him to her, and he would have gone.

She had said no.

The seminarians arose and went to kneel before the Bishop, who laid his hands upon each of their heads in turn, passing the spirit of the priesthood into each. Rob remembered the weight of the Bishop's hands, lightly resting on his head, knowing that the moment had come, that all the power and grace of the centuries poured into him. Every priest since Simon Peter had been ordained by the touch of another, who had also been ordained by the touch of another, all the way back through the line to Jesus himself.

The priests around Rob stood, and he rose and followed them forward to bless the newly ordained. It didn't matter that Jessica had turned him away, though. As much as Rob was attracted to her, even believed that he loved her, if he never saw her again, he would still survive. He already knew how to be lonely. He shuffled closer to the sanctuary in line, his hands folded before him like a good Catholic boy.

He wouldn't go back East to the university and study for his diocese. He would not go to Rome. He would not become a canon lawyer or spend his remaining years holed among files and annulments and broken marriages, though he didn't quite know what else he might do. Jessica still lingered in the back of his mind, no wraith, as real as his own two hands. Someday, somehow, he might even call her. Tell her everything. Marry her.

Thou art a priest forever.

After the ordinations, Rob would speak to the Priest Personnel Director, who stood ten feet ahead of him in line, and tell him, "I'm leaving," words he swore he'd never say again.

Rob waited, and at his turn, approached the four young priests, anointed and new. "May *you* find the peace of Christ in your journey," he whispered to each as he blessed them.

"Amen."

Acknowledgements

This book would not have been possible without the true stories of various unnamed Catholic priests, and pro-ordination nuns who also shared their thoughts and opinions.

A Reader's Guide to *Tongues of Angels*

1. *Tongues of Angels* is about a Catholic priest and his battle with celibacy. The stories are based on true stories from real Catholic priests. Are any of these insider stories familiar to you, as a Catholic or non-Catholic? Do any of these sound real to you?

2. The novel touches upon such varied but timely issues as the ordination of women, misogyny in the Church, ill-considered placement of unsupervised priests with children, the double-standard of celibacy for gay versus straight priests, the code of silence for priestly misbehavior, addiction, and compulsion as reaction to a strict society, and the repressive political and social strictures within the Church. Which seems the most pressing in today's Church? In today's world?

3. Do you find the explanations of different Catholic ceremonies, language, and traditions confusing or enlightening? Can you understand how people are drawn to religion when in deep pain?

4. How does Jessica's story affect you? Do you approve or disapprove of her handling of her rape and abortion, and the aftermath? Is her post-traumatic stress authentic? In your opinion, does she need to seek forgiveness, or do you think she has suffered enough?

5. What does celibacy mean to Rob? What does it mean to Lawrence? What does it mean to Jessica? What does it mean to the Bishop?

6. Author Julia Park Tracey has said in interviews, "The story is about celibacy in the Church, from an insider's perspective. This is not *The Thorn Birds*. It's a literary look at the reality that a Catholic priest faces when he must choose either a celibate life in the priesthood, or a secular life, abandoning his vocation to get married or pursue a relationship." Do you find the novel pro-Church or anti-Church? Does this resonate with you or do you have a different understanding of the theme of the novel?

7. Does the frank portrayal of priests behind doors feel offensive or authentic? Can a person be both profane and spiritual? Are religious people allowed to "blow off steam" or "let down their hair"? Should they need to? Is it a sin?

8. The priests in this fictional diocese act as a support system to each other, but also enforce peer pressure and conformity. As a literary device, the priests are the Greek chorus whose job it is to comment on other drama and action. Who is your favorite priest in the story, and who is your least favorite?

Want more?

If you liked this novel, write a review on Amazon and GoodReads.

"Like" the *Tongues of Angels* page on Facebook.

Follow Julia Park Tracey on Twitter@JuliaParkTracey.
"Like" Julia Park Tracey, Author, on Facebook.

Follow The Doris Diaries on Twitter@TheDorisDiaries.
"Like" The Doris Diaries page on Facebook.

Visit www.juliaparktracey.com for more about Julia Park Tracey.

CPSIA information can be obtained at www.ICGtesting.com
Printed in the USA
BVOW011049200513

321167BV00004B/8/P